Dedicated to my late loving Mother and Father

RUBINDER HOOD PRINCE OF CHORS

BILLY BABU

authorHOUSE®

AuthorHouse™ UK Ltd.
1663 Liberty Drive
Bloomington, IN 47403 USA
www.authorhouse.co.uk
Phone: 0800.197.4150

© 2014 Billy Babu. All rights reserved.

No part of this book may be reproduced, stored in a retrieval system, or transmitted by any means without the written permission of the author.

Published by AuthorHouse 09/09/2014

ISBN: 978-1-4969-9073-0 (sc)
ISBN: 978-1-4969-9074-7 (e)

Any people depicted in stock imagery provided by Thinkstock are models, and such images are being used for illustrative purposes only. Certain stock imagery © Thinkstock.

This book is printed on acid-free paper.

Because of the dynamic nature of the Internet, any web addresses or links contained in this book may have changed since publication and may no longer be valid. The views expressed in this work are solely those of the author and do not necessarily reflect the views of the publisher, and the publisher hereby disclaims any responsibility for them.

Contents

Chapter One:	Rubinder Hood Prince of Chors (Thieves)	1
Chapter Two:	Rubinder & Mere Merion	13
Chapter Three:	Rubinder Hood & the Sóná (gold) Hockey Danda	37
Chapter Four:	Rubinder Hood meets Nikka Johnu	54
Chapter Five:	Rubinder Hood & the Meat Walla	65
Chapter Six:	Rubinder Hood & Raja Resham	90
Chapter Seven:	The Death of Rubinder Hood	103

Chapter One

Rubinder Hood Prince of Chors (Thieves)

Long, long ago, there was a very kind dil (hearted) ruler of India. He was a Raja (King). He was named Resham the Sher Dil (Lion–heart). He was a very noble and approachable Raja with Nawabs (governors) whom he had personally appointed because he was often away on visits and fighting for the Holy Zameen (land/ground).

These "governors" were all very arrogant and lalchi (greedy). They would fight and help the Raja because he had promised to give them rupees (money) and zameen as a reward. Because he was trusting and very busy, the Raja was not aware how lalchi his Nawabs were – so unlike royalty.

The Nawabs were chors (thieves). They stole zameen, makaans (houses), rupees and pasu (cattle) from the pind waley (village people), which they gave to their gharwaley (house family). The pind waley themselves had very often become the servants of these proud Nawabs. Some of these pind waley would sadly sing in the pinds: "Young bandey (men) won't you come out and fight? I said young bandey won't you please come out tonight?" But this never happened. So, it came about that two castes lived in India (namely the high and low). Each Nawab had his own language and they hated one another. Sadly, this is still often the way of life in India, underlined with the 'evil' caste system and as they say: 'More wants more!' This is the only language that they seem to understand. Most bankers would bank on this and never lose interest. I would have been a banker, but I lost interest and I withdrew!

Resham 'The Sher Dil,' as his name tells you, was a brave and noble banda (man). He loved danger, brave bandey and their deeds. He hated all mean, cruel acts and the cowards who carried them out. He was always ready to help the weak against the strong. His bodyguard was always around and he was rightly named "Gol Gappa" (Crispy, round and hollow like a crisp). Everyone could see him coming around and they were able to see straight through him!

Resham taught the proud Nawabs, in a quote, that true nobility rests in: "The fruits of the Spirit are; pyaar (love), joy, peace, patience, kindness, goodness, faithfulness, gentleness and self–control against such things there is no law, not in fierceness and cruelty." This sadly had fallen on deaf kann (ears) because they only had delle (eyes) for themselves and their delle were never satisfied! Delle larger than their dhidd (bellies), now there's sight for saw delle (eyes) or sight for sore eyes?

Yet Resham himself was neither meek nor gentle. He was indeed very courageous and ruthless in battle. Whenever he had a hockey danda (stick), he was very dangerous. He would never back down from fighting with anyone who was stronger or better armed than himself. To Resham, it would have been shameful to show that you were weak and feeble. You could always tell when he was going in to battle because he would ask for his bright lal (red) turban, which he wore with pride. Don't forget what the community may say. Never looking at themselves, but being more than happy to judge! Look around and judge for yourself or not, as the case maybe?

(This could be a case in question or a case to answer, just in-case you are feeling confused by my case, it may be best to drop the case or you may end up being one; a case and that's it in a nut-case.)

Now Resham didn't stay in India. For there was far over the seas a zameen (land/ground) called Valaait (England), Southhall–on–Sea. There our Lord was born, lived and died. Pind waley (village people), of all ages, did think affectionately of that far–off zameen. It was very difficult to get a visa. However, help was on hath (hand) from Mr. Bhisky (Whisky) – friend of professor thōdī (chin) from the kāḷi zameen (Black Country). For two cases of whisky, he could get you a visa. You would be moved by the CSA (Commuting South Asians), if you wanted to get out, then you would pay for one case of whisky. He had a dost (friend) known as Star. For a Euro, there was a tunnel under the Valaaiti (English) Channel. You would end up in a place

Billy Babu

called France. The French never liked the Indian; they only liked frog's legs and snails. PS: Remember, that no scarves are allowed and leaders can have as many mistresses as they like! It's a banda's (man's) world but nothing without a teemi or a kuri (woman/girl), as Jarnail Brown used to sing.

Sadly, the Valaaiti zameen (English land) at this time had fallen into the hath (hands) of the heathen (known as Cockneys). It seemed to the pind waley (village people) in those days that it would be a terrible sin to allow the wicked heathen to live in the Holy Zameen. So, they gathered together up great armies of brave bandey (men) from every zameen (land) in the world and sent them to try and win back the zameen (Ya na what I mean?). Many brave deeds were carried out, many dreadful battles fought, but still the heathen kept possession. This was due to the fact, once they had been captured, no one could decipher their language. It transpired that for stairs they'd say: "Apples and pears." Apple bobbing means: "robbing." To top it off, Robin Hood means: "good," whoever he was? The list goes on! Just like a long–running play that they called "Currynation Street. Starring Khan Baba–low."

Brave Raja Resham of India said: "I will fight for the zameen Valaait of our Lord." So, he gathered together as many rupees as he could muster (you have to muste muste must), as many brave bandey (men) that would follow him and set out for the Holy Zameen (Holy Land). Someone had said there was a tunnel that had been built by the "Iron Lady" and some French banda (man). If this was true then they could use the tunnel, rather than risk landing by ships. (It was common knowledge that the French were always on strike and no one would ask for any ID because there was no one there! By the way, ID stands for Indian dowry). Even the border officers didn't check everybody's paper work. The Thoriyan de teemi (Tory woman) said that this was fine by her. (Also, you can eat toriyan make friends with a Punjabi and invite yourself around for a meal). This will not be the case if the UKIPP (United Kingdom Indian Partying People) take control. It will be all hands up in the air please. (Just check out any Indian party.)

Before the Raja went away, he called two night temple waley (Men who worked in the temple at night). He knew they were good and wise bandey. (The Raja knew he might be away for some time and he couldn't trust many bandey). He said to them: "Take care of India while I am gone. Rule the pind waley (village people) wisely and well. I will reward you on my return."

The night temple waley promised to do as the Raja asked. He then said farewell and sailed away down the River Ganges.

Now, Raja Resham had a half vera (brother) named Prince Javed. (He was good looking from a distance – just like his daughter – ugly Beti). Prince Javed was the opposite in every way to Raja Resham. He was not at all approachable. He was jealous of Resham because he was a Raja (king). He was angry because he'd not been chosen to rule whilst Resham was in Southhall–On–Sea. As soon as Raja Resham had gone, Javed approached the night temple waley (people) and told them: "You must be letting me rule while the Raja is

Billy Babu

away, understanding?" (His Pinglish wasn't berry {very in Punjabi} good).

So the night temple waley allowed him to do so, knowing if they did not allow him, they could then end up in a 'Korma' or have a dodgy 'Tikka.' Deep down in his wicked dil (heart), Javed was out to make himself Raja (king) and never letting Resham come back into India.

A time of great sorrow had now begun for the pind waley (village people). Javed had tried to please the naughty Nawabs (governors) because they were powerful and he hoped they would help to make him Raja. He thought the best way to please them was to give them more zameen (Ya na what I mean?) and pasie (money). Though he had none of his own, he was indeed named Javed Lack–zameen (land), he took it from the pind waley (village people) and gave it to the Nawabs. Thus many of the pind waley once more became homeless beggars (even the takeaways closed), they lived a wild life in the hari lakri (green wood), which covered a great part of India at this time. The greedy USA (Undermining South Asians) hadn't come to exploit the zameen yet.

Now, among the few pind waley who still remained and who had not been choried (robbed) of their zameen (land/ground) and pasie (money), there was one named Rupi, Earl of Dundee (hockey sticks manufacturer). He had one munda (son) also named Rupi the Nikka (little one), but the pind waley called him Rubinder. He sometimes cleaned the bindas (Punjabi windows).

Rubinder Hood Prince of Chors

Rubinder was a favourite with all the pind waley. Tall, strong, handsome and full of fun. Rubinder kept his papa's ghar (house) radiant with music, fun and laughter. He was valiant and courageous too. There was no better hockey player in all the zameen (land). This was due to Rubinder eating his greens – his saag aloo (spinach and potato), but not too much as they wanted to keep the hara ghar (green house) gases in check! With it all, he was mild and kind dil–walla (hearted), never hurting the frail or stole from the needy. You could always spot Rubinder coming because he wore a beautiful hari (green) turban and he was never without it.

There was a party at the Earl's ghar (house) and all his gharwāley and dosts (Family and friends) were invited. Rubinder was dancing with everyone, with their hath (hands) in the air. Rubinder called his papa over and said to him: "Come papa Ji, let's see if you've still got the best moves or do I have them all now?"

Papa Ji (The Earl of Dundee) shouted back: "Oh, no, no, you having them now my munda, burrwahh burrwahh," and everyone laughed. They all shouted: "Burrwahh!" ('Burrwahh' can't be done if you don't have a top lip. Instead, you should sing: "All my life I've been kissing your bottom lip, cos the top one's missing: Oh Boy! Or girl? To be PC").

It was getting late and all the guests were starting to leave and fill their phandey (dishes) with left over chapattis, pillow rice (somewhere to rest their heads) and dhal (vegetarian dish). Nobody had invented the kuttā jholi (doggy bag)

Billy Babu

yet! Now there's a bhhaunkda (barking) mad idea. Or am I bhhaunkda up the wrong tree?

It was now one o'clock in the morning as the Earl Rupi said goodnight to the last of his guests, he yawned and turned to the servants: "Please be putting the jinda (lock) on because I going bed now. If you're wanting party, then please be carrying on." (Isn't 'Carry on' a good name for a play?)

The cock started to crow at three o'clock in the morning but no one heard it, they had eaten so much that they were all sleeping soundly. All the candles were out. (The one candle had said to the other one that he was going out tonight). The only ones that were awake, sucking the khoon (blood) and biting everyone, were the mosquitoes! (They were training to become Nawabs or members of parliament – with expenses?) You could hear all the loud snoring and burping all over the pind. All the kuttey (dogs) were howling and billiyan (cats) were crying. This meant that there was death in the air, or at least that is the superstition that is believed in India. To see a kalli billi (black cat) is not good news – a bit like a banker's bonus or MP's expense bill.

Now, the Earl of Dundee had a bitter enemy and that night his enemy the Sherif of Not–eating–ham, (who was sometimes called Oh–My–Sherif), came with his bandey (men). The Sherif was determined to kill the earl and take all his sóná (gold) and zameen (land). The Sherif of Not–eating–ham with his bandey attacked the ghar (home) of the Earl of Dundee and there was a fierce and terrible battle, but in the end Rupi and all his bandey were killed. His ghar (home) was burned to the zameen (ground) and all his paise (money) stolen. Only Rubinder was saved. Sadly, his favourite kuttā (dog) Lassi (Named because of his pyaar (love) of sweet milk) was killed too. Rubinder fought bravely, but as he saw his Papa Ji's ghar in flames, he had no dil (heart) to fight any longer.

So, Rubinder took his hockey danda (stick) and he fled to the great hari lakri (green wood). He went on khora–back (horse back) as fast as his khora would carry him, for the Sherif's bandey (men) were close behind him. Soon, he reached the edge of the hari lakri but he knew he had to keep going, deeper and deeper under the canopy of the trees. He then came to a place where he felt he could rest and he lay on the hara khaa (green grass). He was trying to control his breathing but it seemed to take forever to catch his breath. Rubinder lost consciousness and soon fell into a deep sleep.

When he awoke, Rubinder's dil (heart) felt as if it was burning. He was full of anger and violent thoughts of revenge that were tearing him up. He was feeling very embittered. These evil bandey (men) had, in one moment of cruelty, taken everything away from him: his papa Ji, his ghar, servants, pasu, bakree (cows and goats), zameen, rupees, burnt the hockey shop and even his name. They were all gone. He would never be the next Earl – just another pind walla (village man).

Rubinder was battered, famished and exhausted. As he lay with his bootha (face) against the cool hara khaa (green grass), he grasped the supple, moist moss with his hath (hand). It was not grief or pain he felt, but only a bitter longing for revenge. He felt a sense of warmth from the great old tree and other somber trees waved gently overhead in the warm breeze. The setting of the sun sent shafts of golden glimmers light into the breezy, blue shade. Birds sang their nightfall songs, deer rustled softly through the underlakree (under wood) and bright–eyed squirrels leaped noiselessly from branch to branch. His khora (horse) had found some pāṇī (water) to quench its thirst. There was serenity and tranquility everywhere except in poor Rubinder's heated dil (heart).

Rubinder had always loved the hari lakree (green wood). He loved the scent, the views, the sounds and the deep calmness of it. It brought back thoughts of his bachéhood (childhood) and the warmth of it all filled him up with emotion. He reminisced how he would be brought into the hari lakri on the tanga (horse and cart) and how wonderful it was. But the baché (children) of today didn't call it tanga anymore; they now called it tan–go. This was due to the baché of today wanting to be suntanned and have an orange tan, while they'd be out riding in the sun. How times had changed! At one time, no Indian would want to be out in the sun – due to the fear of becoming dark and being type–casted!

Rubinder remembered how he had collected lakri (wood) for his papa Ji. At this thought he had pāṇī (tears) running from his delle (eyes) and the sobbing made him quiver, as he lay on the hara khaa (green grass). The bitterness and rage had all drained out of his dil (heart), only sadness and emptiness encompassed what was once a joyful dil. How he longed for yesterday; pyaar (love) was such an easy hockey game to play, now he needed a place to hide away, oh, he so longed for yesterday – he thought. This was one of his favorite songs from the kāḷā (black) Beatle album.

As night time drew near it was beginning to over shadow him. In the twilight of the evening, Rubinder knelt down and prayed. Then, with one hath on his turban and the other on his dil (heart), he stood up and swore an oath. This was the oath:

"I swear to pyaar (love) God and the Raja,

to help the frail and fight the evil and

to take from the wealthy and give to the deprived.

I will be always pyaaring, approachable and respectful as my

earthly papa Ji was and do what is right for India.

I will take no notice of pagals (fools) that call anyone a loser.

May God help me with His authority."

Rubinder felt it had been a hard day's night and he had been riding like a kuttā (dog). Rubinder was emotionally drained and needed to rest. He lay on the hara khaa (green grass) under the trees with his favourite hockey danda beside him and he fell into another deep sleep. As he slept, the deer, squirrels, rabbits, donkeys and birds all fell silent to ensure that Rubinder had a restful sleep. It was as if they were aware of the calling upon his jaan (life) and the support of all the living creatures in the hari lakri (green wood) that he would require.

(Remember: It's bad when you forget things you should really remember and it's sad when you remember things you're supposed to forget. Don't let the zeher (poison) of loki (people's) words and actions take up your time.)

So a lassi (cold sweet milky drink), here starts the adventures of the famous "Rubinder Hood of the Sherlakree" (Sherwood).

Chapter Two
Rubinder & Mere Merion

Once upon time there was a beautiful kuri (girl), who lived in the pind (village) and her papa was the Nawab (governor). Her name was Mere (my) Merion. She was not allowed out and had to wear a chunni (veil). Many pind waley (village people) had never been graced by her beauty. Merion was twenty years old. She wanted to go out and see the pinds (villages), but her papa wouldn't allow this. He wanted her to stay in and sew the kameez (shirts), so that he could sell them at the kāḷā (black) country bazaar (market). Poor Merion, all she wanted was to go shopping and meet some new loki (people) who would loki out for her. But her papa didn't want her to get into any trouble. So she was not going any place; just staying in. This was the safest place for her and the safest place was the rasoi (kitchen). They do say a kuri's (girls) work is never done? Won't cook, can't cook – oh you will learn.

One day, Merion's aunty came to their ghar (home). Merion's aunty was going to the Mindo (bingo Punjabi style). She was going on her own and wamted someone to accompany her.

Billy Babu

"Oh please papa Ji can I go? I won't let you down," begged Merion, with her hath (hands) together.

"No! Not a chance and don't be asking me again!"

His bootha (face) was saara (burnt). This was due to being out in the sun on his tanga, which the kids called tan–go. You can get a tan–on–the–go!

Merion ran off to her room, her papa's voice reverberating in her kan (ears). Her papa was shouting at Merion's aunty, saying she was going to spoil his beti (daughter) just like she had spoilt her own beti – who was now divorced, had two baché (children) and now living at her bebe's (mother's) ghar (house).

(Once you've had a beti (daughter) who was divorced, it was not only shame on the family but also shame on the pind (village). No one would give you their munda (son) in shaadi (marriage), even if the kuri wasn't to blame). That's why it's a safe bet to keep your beti ghar (home). Oh Beti, the kuta's caused a woopsy!

Mere Merion had heard everything and began to sob. She loved her papa, but was fed up with him covering her up in cotton wool. He had to realize that she wasn't a baché (child), she was now a grown–up. Then, there was a knock on her bedroom buhaa (door). It was her papa.

"Merion, I am knowing you're upset. Please don't crying you stupie baché (stupid child). If you really want to be going and be having game of Mindo then I won't be standing in your way. But please remember, I wanting to be able to show my chēhrā (face) in the pind. (He was the chereman of the local committee – self-elected like most of them). If you be letting me down, and making me look stupie, then I will be having a saara bootha (burnt face). Come, be going with your aunty Ji, she's waiting downstairs." Papa ji said with a big smile on his bootha – twirling his moustache, this was his hobby, most of the cats liked this hobby of his. Nine out of ten cats preferred his bhiskers (Punjabi whiskers).

Merion couldn't believe what she had just heard! She jumped up and hugged her papa Ji and twirled his bhiskers (and why not).

"Oh papa Ji, thank you so much, I won't let you down, it's so nice to just go out for once in my jaan (life)." Merion said, with a grin as wide as a Cheshire Billie (err, cat from up north Punjab).

Merion and her aunty got onto the tanga (horse and carriage) and rode out as the gates were opened, Merion saw the outside after such a long time and she was taken aback. Merion hadn't seen the outside since her last day at school. All she had ever heard were the sounds of the horns, the pind waley's (village people) shouting and their spitting. They didn't pass through the hari lakri (green wood_ because this would have been dangerous. They followed two Indians; Sat and Nav (aka Satvinder and Navinder) because they knew the quickest way to the local Mindo hall – down the GT road (fast road in the Punjab).

Billy Babu

"So, this is what it's like on the outside?" Merion shouted as the wind was blowing her chunni over her bootha (face). She pushed her hair back in place because she didn't want to have a bad hair day.

"Yes, my dear niece, and it's not all good. Sadly, there are a lot of bad things out in this world and then there are bandey (men). But I tell you now that if there were no bad teemiyan (women) there would be no bad bandey!" Laughed aunty Ji, as she checked out all the bandey. Keeping a della (eye) out for her niece?

"What's wrong with bandey? My papa Ji is a banda (man) and we have a few pind waley (village men) who come to work on our zameen (land) and there are no problems." Merion asked, with her máthá (forehead) all creased up.

"Oh, my poor nikki beti (little daughter). You're so innocent and that makes it even more dangerous for you!" Aunty Ji said while was still looking around at all the bandey (men).

"But, I don't understand, and I'm a fast learner. Would you teach me, aunty Ji?" Merion asked with a heavenly innocence.

"I'm still learning my sweet baché (daughter) and I've been around for years! So, please let's forget this pagal (barmy) conversation. Oh look, here's the Mindo (bingo) hall. Let's enjoy Mindo for tonight and then we can pick up on this conversation again," Merion's aunty said, with a concerned look and a frown; as she searched frantically for her batuya (purse).

Rubinder Hood Prince of Chors

The Mindo hall was packed with pind waley (village people) from all the local pinds (villages). Before you had even entered into the Mindo hall, there were sellers of every description there, aiming to get your paisa (money) off you.

There were sabji walla (vegetable seller), hajamat walla (barber), darjee (tailor), kulfi walla (ice cream) and Cholay Baturay walla (chick peas, and chapatti). Horns sounding, the punka walla (fanning man) and of course the mosquitoes, sucking the khoon (blood) out of everyone – just like the Punjab police – chai paani! (Tea and water).

As they went in, Merion heard the Mindo caller: "delle down," (eyes down).

Everyone had a jar of nimbu ka achar (lemon pickle) that they used to dab on the numbers and when they had full ghar (house), they would shout: "Oi." This was to instruct one of the assistances to come over and check the numbers. They'd win a prize, which could be a kabutar (pigeon), bakree (goat) or the top prize of a pasu (cow). Many bandey would laugh and say that they already had one at ghar (home)!

Here are some of the Punjabi Mindo (bingo) numbers:

1 Kelly's Eye – Kaaliya di akh (or della)
3 Cup of Tea – Charlie cup of cha
4 Knock at the Door – buhey te kat-kat
5 Man Alive – zinda aadmi
9 Doctor's orders – doctor da hukum
10 David's Den – David th Ghar (only till 2015?)

11 Legs Eleven – gyara latta
12 One Dozen – Ikk-darjen
17 Dancing Queen – nachanwali rani (but not from abbaa ji)
18 Coming of Age – burappa
21 Key of the Door – buhey di chabbi
22 Two Little Ducks – do batka
24 Two Dozen – duo darjen
33 Dirty Knee – gandey goddey
40 Naughty Forty – eltha chali
45 Halfway There – addey rastey
88 Two Fat Ladies – do mothiyan teemiyan (not very PC)
90 Top of the Shop – dukaan dey uppar

Merion and her aunty didn't win anything. They had lost all the paise (money) that she had in her batuya (purse). Now, her dear aunty didn't want to leave. Instead, she carried on playing by borrowing paise from her dosts (friends) and built up a large debt. Poor Merion, her first day out was turning into a disaster. She knew that if she stayed any longer then her papa would not be happy and if she went back on her own, her aunty would be in trouble – what was she to do? (This is becoming a real drama oh dearie me.)

"Aunty, I have to go. You know we have been here far too long," begged Merion. But her aunty was in gambling mode and had caught the evil bug of spend, spend, spend. Merion got up licking the nimbu ka achar (lemon pickle) from her stained unggli (finger) and walked towards the exit sign she knew it was getting late.

Rubinder Hood Prince of Chors

Merion called the tangey walla (horse and cart man) over and asked him to take her ghar (home). Sat and Nav were not there due to Indian timing!

"Oh yes, please. But where is your aunty Ji?"

"She's not coming. I need to get back now! So can we go Tangey walla?"

So off they went. The sun was setting, the wind was building up and the dark clouds were gathering. (With that sort of forecast, I should have been a weather man, my teacher told me I should because I could never get anything right at school.)

As they raced towards the pind, trying to miss the pot holes and the Punjab Police, they had to divert through the hari lakri (green wood) (They didn't have any paise for chai paani; the Punjab Police. Of course not forgetting the other blood suckers – mosquitoes! There is an old Indian saying; bring your batuya (purse) and we will help empty it for you!)

As they raced through the hari lakri (green wood), they could hear the sound of khoray (horses) approaching from the rear. They didn't look back, but just kept going.

"Oi you! Stop or I will stop you with my hockey danda!" Shouted the voice from the kāḷāness (darkness) of the lakree (wood).

Billy Babu

They pulled over with dils (hearts) pounding. The tangey walla asked: "Hello please. What can I be doing for you on this hot evening?" (His head was rocking from side to side).

"You can be giving me all the rupees you have or I will be letting you taste my hockey danda all over your body," sneered the vada banda (big man).

"I don't be having any rupees. I'm just be taking Nawab's kuri (governor's daughter) back to ghar (home). Please be letting us go and may our god bless you a thousand times," said the tangey walla whilst shaking in his kenchi chapla (scissors flip flops).

"Hmmm, that's better still, a rich kuri (girl). Well, forget your rupees; we will get a lot more from her papa Ji. So, you can go and give him the message!" Laughed the vada banda and his two accomplices – who had now joined him.

One of the bandey (men) pulled Merion off the tanga. She was too stunned to say or do anything – as she had never had contact with any banda (man) before. She was thinking about what would her poor papa Ji have to do? He had warned her how evil the outside was. She carried out all the requests of these chors (thieves) and kept her chunni over her bootha (face).

As the tangey walla rode off into the kāḷā lakree (dark wood), he didn't look back because he was frightened for his own jaan (life), he wasn't happy being cowardly. He was lost and he didn't have his two Indian dosts (friends), good old Sat and Nav (Satvinder and Navinder), with him to show him the way back.

"So, my soni kuri (pretty girl), what shall we do? While we wait for your very rich papa Ji, what shall we all do to entertain ourselves?" Smirked the vada banda to his bandey – they all laughed.

Now, unbeknown to Merion and the kidnappers, Rubinder was out practicing his swing (not through the trees, but with his hockey swing). He heard all the laughing and thought someone must be having a late bahbi–cook (Sister–in–law cooking on a barbecue).

As Rubinder approached them he could see this was no bahbi–cook, but three bandey who looked like chors. He climbed up the nearest tree – maybe he was swinging after all – so he could get a good view and find out what was going on here. He heard their plans to hold the kuri for ransumjit (Punjabi type of ransom).

Rubinder came down from the tree and pulled out his hockey danda that he had just been polishing. He was going to knock some heads together and maybe damage his danda as these chors looked like real thick heads! (I could have put something else – but didn't want to make a Richard of myself).

All of a sudden you heard dusham, dusham! (whack whack) All the bandey (men) were on the zameen (ground). (Not Bob Marley type – I want to zameen, I want to zameen with you).

Billy Babu

Rubinder asked a stunned Merion, who was hiding her bootha: "How are you?"

"I, I'm fine thank you," replied Merion. "Are you a doctor? Asking me if I'm all right?"

"Well, I'm not a doctor but you know it's what everyone asks everyone – whether they mean it or not? Now, let's get you out of this kāḷā lakree (dark wood) and back to your gharwaley (family)," said Rubinder who was wiping the sweat off his máthá (forehead).

Rubinder took Merion's hath (hand) and put her onto his khora (horse). "Hold tight!" Rubinder shouted, as they galloped off. The chors were still out cold as Rubinder's khora kicked dust into their boothe (faces). Who knows? A local security firm may pick them up and lock them up – Gurpal Sodi Four the job? (GS4).

(If you like that link-up, please tag someone in, but not on a false leg.)

As they rode towards Merion's ghar, she had to hold Rubinder firmly. Merion had never spoken to a strange banda (man) but here she was holding a stranger and she had a feeling in her dil (heart) that she had never felt before. Was Merion falling in love? She not only felt comfort from holding onto this handsome banda but she also loved the warmth of his body next to hers. They didn't kiss because this is not allowed in India.

Rubinder Hood Prince of Chors

Finally, after some Indian travelling time, they arrived at Merion's ghar (home). They asked two Indians the way – good old Sat and Nav – if they had children they could name them Tom–u Tom–u and Sarmin?

Merion greeted her papa Ji, explaining to her papa what had happened and how this banda (man) had saved her from the chors in the hari lakri (green wood). The Nawab turned towards Rubinder and said: "I am thank you banda (man) for saving my only kuri (daughter). You can be having whatever you wanting."

"I don't need anything Nawab Ji. It was an honour to be of service." Rubinder replied as he tried not to look at Merion.

"Well, you be must come to the dinna (Punjabi dinner) this Sunda (Punjabi Sunday). We be having a feast and invite some of our dosts as well. To be giving thanks for the safe return of my Merion and I get the Sherif to be catching these chors (thieves)!" Replied the Nawab with a joyful voice, covering the undertone of his anger. He wanted to bend the chors over and make them hold their kann (ears); a punishment that is still mete out to this day – but not by the vegetarians of India.

As Rubinder and Papa Ji were talking, a tanga pulled up. It was the aunty. She was lal (red) in the bootha (face) because she knew she was going to be told off by the Nawab. But he didn't say anything other than giving her a stern look. On the whole, he was happy to have his beti (girl) back – with her honour!

Billy Babu

Rubinder said: "My dear Nawab, it's time for me to go now. I will be honoured to share a meal with you." As he said this, he looked over at Merion and smiled. Merion looked at Rubinder and blushed. She could blush easily because she was very fair. (I have to say this to be fair). If she had been out in the sun then she would have been darker and it would have been more difficult to ascertain if she was blushing – as she pulled her chunni over her bootha (face).

So, the Nawab sent for his bandey (men). He told them to start sending out invitations to all the vadey bandey (big men) of the pind and ask Delhi Smith to start the cooking. Delhi Smith was a famous cook from Port Blair where they housed Indian convicts, mostly political prisoners. It is also known as "Kāḷā Pāṇī" translated as Black Waters because they do say politics is a "dirty business."

As Rubinder went off on his khora (horse), his dil (heart) was beating very fast – he was falling in pyaar (love) and he knew Merion must be feeling the same way. When Rubinder got back to his camp, his bandey (men) asked him what happened. As ever, he told the story but with a little bit of mirch (chili) added to spice up the tale! As always, they went to sleep before he had finished his tale!

Back at Merion's ghar (house), her head was spinning. She spoke to some of her gharwaley (family) about this and they were all very excited about the party. Especially excited that Rubinder would be the guest of honour – but no one knew that Rubinder was a "wanted" banda (man). All the pind waley (village people) and Rubinder's bandey (men) would take down all the drawings of Rubinder, so not many knew what he looked like. There was a naughty son who was like news of dunia (world) – he would hack into any tree to listen in and sell your story to Rupi Mud–Rock. A newspaper besharam (one with no shame).

The beekend (Punjabi weekend) came and Rubinder was excited. All the guests started to arrive and as good Punjabi's, they didn't eat at their own ghar (home). They would fill themselves at the party! There is always a "Phukha" (hungry) family. They have one munda (son) and one beti (daughter) – always ready for a party!

The horns were blasting and tangas (carts) were stuck in the mud but the pind waley (village people) were still coming for free khaana peena (food and drink).

Now, Rubinder was guest of honour and he knew it. However, he was afraid someone may recognise him and shout: "chor!" There was no need to worry about this because all the vadey bandey (important men) would all fit that description, not forgetting the Punjab police – who have a license to steal. Also not forgetting all the politicians, if they stayed overnight, may claim it as their second ghar (home)!

Rubinder came with three of his bandey (men) because he didn't want to attract attention to himself – other than that of Merion. As Rubinder approached Merion's ghar, he informed his bandey to stay out of the way unless there was trouble then they could blow the horn and for them to make a way out for him. So, a plan was worked out and they would also fill their dhidd (stomachs) too. He told them not to get confused with the horn of the rag and haddi (bone) banda (man).

Merion was watching from her binda (Punjabi window) and saw Rubinder approach from the gate where he was taken in. Now, sadly for Rubinder, he would have to sit with the bandey (men) and Merion would have to sit with the teemiyan (women). Due to the crowds of pind waley (village people), Merion lost sight of Rubinder but he was a chor (thief). He knew she had seen him and he made sure that he would sit at the nearest table to the teemiyan. He would have to be careful as the evil Sherif of Nott–Eating–Ham would be there and if he recognised Rubinder then there would be turmoil. Rubinder, thankfully, is a common name as most of them are but they are not as handsome as him – maybe in the dark?

Rubinder went in and made his way to the table that was nearest to the teemiyan (women). Not a lot of bandey (men) would do this as they would usually head towards the khaana peena (food and drink). Rubinder sat there and waited for his rani (queen) to walk into the hall.

As Rubinder was making idle chit chat – please don't confuse for kitu the katu – everyone stopped and looked up. There was Merion, looking like a fairy princess. She wore an underdress of glittering lal (red), over it a robe of lovely satin, hara (green) that shimmered like beech leaves in early spring. Her dark hair was caught up in a net of pearls and a soft white veil fell about her bootha (face). Rubinder drew in his breath. He had not known that anyone could look so beautiful. She looked like a magnificent star. She seemed to glide across the floor, her bootha veiled as it was the custom in those days, but everyone could still tell she was special. Her dress was so stunning. She positioned herself, so that she could see her banda (man).

Then the Nawab came in and with him the Sherif of Nott–Eating–Ham. They sat at the main table and the feast began. There were dancers, dhol waley on the main stage entertaining everyone. Then the MC (money counter) announced the top entertainer of the evening. It was Bob Dhillon.

He had been going for years and all the pind waley loved him – they knew the times are a changing but he will keep singing.

The food and wine were flowing freely. Everyone seemed happy. Rubinder could see his rani (queen) and she could see him. Then the MC got up and asked everyone to mu–bannd (be quiet) as the Nawab was going to make a speech.

The Nawab said: "I am wanting to be thanking young banda (man) who been making me the happiest banda in the whole of Punjab and not being for him, my dear sweet kuri (girl) could have been killed. I am wanting to call him over and presenting him gift. Come here young banda (man) and remove scarf, so can be seeing how handsome you are." However, Rubinder kept it on as he walked over to the Nawab's table. As Rubinder approached the table, he began to sweat, what if the evil Sherif of Nott–Eating–Ham recognised him? How would he get out of this one? And in front of his Merion!

Billy Babu

Rubinder, being the master of disguise, only removed the scarf from his mouth and kept his delle (eye) brows covered. Also, he was not wearing his hari (green) turban. The Nawab gave him a sóná mundre (ring) and beautiful turban. The Nawab shook his hath (hand) and hugged him. Now, Rubinder wanted a more precious gift than this, he had to make his move before the moment would pass.

"My dear Nawab Ji, I am grateful for your hospitality and the respect you've shown me but I don't want any of these gifts. All I would want from you is the hath (hand) of your kuri (daughter) and I would pyaar (love) and honour her for the rest of my jaan (life)."

The whole place went quiet. The Nawab looked shocked. It was only the Sherif of Nott–Eating–Ham who got up and asked: "That's all very well for you to ask such a vada banda (big man), such a request from my dost (friend) but what I want to know is who your papa is? And what caste are you?"

You could hear a pin–du drop. Rubinder knew his papa may have been a vada banda at one time. But now he was dead and someone would point out he had married a teemi (woman) who was the kuri of a barber. So, he wouldn't be seen as a munda (son) of a vada banda but one of a barber. (At school Rubinder was known as barba kāḷā (black) sheep).

"Well, I am waiting!" Shouted the Sherif of Nott–Eating–Ham as he crossed his arms. His bootha was becoming lal (red) and his delle (eyes) were burning through Rubinder's hot, sweaty bootha (face).

"I am not going to lie. I am the munda (son) of a land owner and a barber. I don't have a ghar (home) but I am working to buy one soon," replied a deflated Rubinder. He knew the shaadi–waadi (Rock & Roll marriage) would never happen now and all because of the evil caste system. (I don't want to "cast" dispersions but he is right.)

The whole place erupted with laughter at Rubinder. How could someone so low expect to have a shaadi–waadi with someone who was at the top of the tree? (Never look up at those at the top of a tree because you may have something land on your head.) Rubinder replaced the gifts on the table and turned to walk away, but the Nawab placed his hath on his modha (shoulder) and said: "My dear munda, I would be letting such a loving, caring, approachable munda (boy) like you shaadi–waadi my kuri but what community saying yaar (friend)?" He shook Rubinder's hath – this was to say thanks but no thanking you.

(Remember: People and their actions do not upset us, rather we upset ourselves by BELIEVING their evil can upset us).

Rubinder took one last look at his Merion as he would probably never see her bootha (face) again, sadly too many pind waley (village people) had heard what had been said, and the Sherif of Nott–Eating–Ham would certainly make sure the Nawab wouldn't go back on his word. (And remember your word is your bond. If you don't keep it, it will make an ass of you! Ask anyone from the Punjab. But don't ask James).

Billy Babu

With earnest forgiveness in his delle (eyes), Rubinder turned to the sherif: "God bless you," hoping in faith that God would deal with this besharam (shameless one).

(Remember, a loser will focus on what journey they're going through. A winner will focus on where they're going onto and falling in love is easy. Staying in love is a challenge, letting go is the hardest).

Rubinder wrote a dil–felt (heart felt) letter to Merion:

"When someone you pyaar (love) becomes a memory, the memory becomes a treasure. I shall pyaar you always but this jaan (life) is too difficult for us to be together. So I will let you get on with your jaan. May you find someone from a higher caste and be happy." Merion was very sorrowful when she had read Rubinder's letter. She cried for days. Would her dil (heart) ever heal? Or would she have to attend Papu–worth hospital for broken dils (hearts)?

Sad and lonely now her entire world seemed kāḷā (dark) and dreary. It seemed as if the sun had elapsed and the birds had forgotten to sing. They do say the sun will shine and the birds will sing one day for everyone. Only the kāḷā (black) bird sang – and she didn't sing that well!

(One year later)

As time passed, the feeling for Merion's true pyaar (love) – Rubinder, just grew stronger and stronger. She still respected her papa but she hated the evil caste system and knew it wouldn't be long before her papa would shaadi–waadi her

Rubinder Hood Prince of Chors

off. She didn't want anyone but Rubinder. This still goes on today but not forgetting to please the community!

One day, while her gharwaley (family) were busy carrying on with their own beegness (Punjabi business), Merion disguised herself as a banda (man). She had been drinking a lot of dudh (milk) – it tends to coat your throat depending on the fat content. The result a deeper voice. You na what I mean Hari?

Merion slipped out and rode off into the hari lakri (green wood). As she journeyed further and deeper, her dil (heart) beating faster and faster she felt doubt pulling her back to the comfort of her ghar (house) but her dil wouldn't let her turn back. Whatever the day would bring, she wanted to keep going until she met her jaan (love), Rubinder.

Rubinder was very fond of disguising himself. He was very inventive. Often his dearest dosts (friends) didn't recognise him when they met him dressed like someone else. He never dresses up when he's cross.

As Merion rode through the strange surrounding, she heard a voice and froze: "Oi, you! Who are you? Don't you know no one passes through the hari lakri (green wood) without paying my tax? What is your name and where are you going, munda? (boy)."

Merion was very frightened. Rubinder's voice sounded so stern and hideous that she was unable to recognise it. She could not see his bootha (face) and without saying a word, Merion drew her hockey danda. She was prepared to

Billy Babu

fight to the death for her honour but most importantly the community – don't forget the damn community! Remember the communities are people who are happy to judge you and talk about you but they will never look at themselves.

"Oh? You want to fight? You must be a trainee chor (thief)? Fight then, munda."

Rubinder drew his hockey danda (stick) and the fight began. Though Rubinder was taller and stronger than Merion, she used her danda (stick) well. Rubinder was finding it difficult to get the better of her. He admired the skill and grace with which she defended herself. But his strength and quickness was too much for her and he gave such a low swing that she was swept off her feet, not in the usual way. Rubinder quickly went down to her and forgot the evil voice of his character and spoke in his own voice. When Merion heard it, she grabbed him with both hands and with a cry of delight: "Rubinder, Rubinder," was all she could say. (There is always a lot of echo in Indian plays or do they like to repeat themselves?)

"Merion, Merion," (here we go again), Rubinder replied full of joy. "Merion, can it really be you? Oh, why did you not speak before? I have hurt you!" He added in great distress. Merion removed her scarf, so that he might see it was indeed his own true pyaar (love). Her bootha was gora (fair). There was a smile on her bolh (lips) and her delle (eyes) were full with pāṇī (tears) of joy.

Without a single touch of each other, they laughed, cried and embraced (sorry you can't even visualize kissing – see any Indian play). They hadn't seen each other for over a year. They went to the Ganges to bathe Merion's wound on her ankle. Lovingly, Rubinder bathed and bound up Merion's wound. All the time they laughed and talked. Merion found that the pain was easing from her ankle.

When Merion had finished her story how she had run away, she finished off saying: "I shall die if you leave me to live in the hari lakri (green wood)."

Rubinder replied: "Mithidil." (sweetheart).

Rubinder continued to explain: "I never mean to go away again. I am going to stay with you always. When I was walking alone, I wished that I was coming to the end of the walk but since you started walking with me, my wish is this walk never ends and we will be together forever. Dearest, it is a rough, uncomfortable jaan (life) not fit for a teemi (woman) like you."

"Oh Rubinder, do not make me cry again. My world is a kāḷā (dark) and lonely place when I am away from you. Please let me stay?"

"Well, if you want to stay then it has to be for zindagi (life) and that in my delle (eyes) and in God's this means that you will have to shaadi–waadi me."

"Rubinder Hood? Yes, I would pyaar (love) to be your mithi–gharwali (sweet wife – I can't say I've met many)."

Billy Babu

"Well, I better gather all my bandey (men). Let's get the ceremony on the way, then party! At least we don't have to think of making a list of the invites; so and so won't come because so and so is going to be there!" Rubinder laughed.

Rubinder and Merion had only been shaadi (married) for one month when the Sherif of Nott–Eating–Ham found out. He was very jealous; he'd always wanted Merion to be his. Shamed and disgraced the Sherif of Nott–Eating–Ham vowed if he couldn't have her then no one would.

One summer's day, Rubinder and his bandey (men) were out maching (fishing) and Merion went to the pind (village) fashion show that was being hosted by Ikk (one) Goka. Merion was spotted in the crowd and a message was relayed to the Sherif of Nott–Eating–Ham. He asked one of his bandey (men) to call Vinga Dale (Bent Dale). He was so bent that he had asked the pind waley (village people) to give him a rupee till he was straight – which was never! They wouldn't give him one but I know a banda (man) who will!

The Sherif of Nott–Eating–Ham said to Vinga Dale: "I want Merion out of the way and I want her death to look like an accident."

Merion had gone with three of her dosts (friends) to the fashion show. To have his own way, Vinga Dale would bribe or do any bent deals with anyone. Vinga Dale could see that they would be having a drink of pāṇī (water) as the day was very hot.

Rubinder Hood Prince of Chors

Vinga Dale knew that the pāṇī walla (water seller) was very popular; he was able to make "holy water," he would do this by boiling the Hell out of it! He went over to the pāṇī walla (water seller) and asked him to administer some zeher (poison) into their silver plated cups. If the pāṇī walla carried out his instructions then he would look after him, but if he failed to carry out his orders then Vinga Dale would have his license removed via the Punjab police – the choice was his.

Sadly, the pāṇī walla (water- man not Pete) did as he was ordered and administered the zeher (poison). He gave Merion and her dosts the pāṇī at half price. (He felt guilty charging them the full price.) He would have used his poisonous snake, thus removing himself from the crime but sadly the snake had bitten its own tongue and died!

(Merion and her dosts happily paid half price for the pāṇī (water). They walked to the grassed area for teemiyan (women) and sat down to drink their pāṇī, not knowing this would be the last drink they would all have. About twenty minutes later they all fell ill and were taken to the Rani's (queens) medical centre, where they sadly all passed away the following day.)

After the burial of his dear Merion, Rubinder was left to pick up the pieces of his shattered dil (heart) and jaan (life) and move on. Not just for his sake but his honour of the ghar (house hold) name, his dosts (friends), and the pind waley (village people). Not forgetting the community!

Billy Babu

Rubinder Hood never found out who had given the zeher (poison) to his dear Merion and her dosts – he had a good idea but no proof. As they say: "The proof of the pudding is in the eating." He wasn't going to eat zeher (poison)!

Rubinder never shaadi (married) again and never had another pyaar (love) in his jaan (life) again. He just threw himself into helping others and found comfort and joy from this. Rubinder knew, in his dil (heart), that one day he and his true pyaar would be together in heaven with their Lord.

Chapter Three

Rubinder Hood & the Sóná (gold) Hockey Danda

The Sherif of Nott–eating–ham tried to seize Rubinder many times but failed (Rubinder being a master of disguise and a chor).

The more he failed, the angrier (not good for the BP) he became until the kāḷāness (blackness) filled all his dil (heart). "Rubinder Hood dead," was the only head–line he wanted to read in the newspapers.

The Sherif of Nott–eating–ham knew that he would have to ask the Nawabs if they would let him have some of their bandey (men). This is the only way he would stand a chance against the mighty Rubinder. The Sherif of Nott–eating–ham would tell them that he was doing them a "Curry favour." He wanted Rubinder to eat one of his hot curries, he would then have the runs – something the Valaait (England) cricket team would love!

Billy Babu

The Nawabs had been fighting in the Holy Zameen (land) of Southhall–On–Sea. They didn't trust the Sherif but they also didn't have a lot of time for Rubinder – as he was robbing them of their paise (money).

One day, the Sherif of Nott–eating–ham set out for a meeting with all the Nawabs. He took his bandey (men) and his best tanga (horse and carriage). It took him many days to reach Southhall–On–Sea, due to the many check points; these were staffed – not manned, it's not PC – by the Punjab police and the Euro border agency staff. They like to ask if you have any chai paani (tea and water) – so you could say that you've been choried (robbed) "legally or not illegally." You can decide. The Euro border agency was always on duty but they didn't check everybody's details. Their boss said that they didn't have to do this all the time. Well you know what they say: "When the billi (cat) is away the chewe (mice) will play." Somehow, I don't see this working out and there may be an enquiry into the everyday banda (man) in the pind (village) having to pay for this enquiry - Oh, what a surprise!

The Sherif of Nott–eating–ham had taken extra bandey (men) on this trip for the following reasons: there would be many chors (thieves) on the way and it was going to take a week to get there. The Sherif of Nott–eating–ham needed his bandey to keep dek–da (watch) at night. This is the time the chors would attack in kāḷāness (darkness) whilst they slept.

Late on the seventh day, the Sherif of Nott–eating–ham arrived in Southhall-on-Sea. He was very tired after his

Rubinder Hood Prince of Chors

long journey. He was thankful to his saali (sister in law) who would read his bootha (face) and told him he would be choried (robbed) legally – the Punjab police? His saali did find it difficult to read his saara bootha (miserable face). She was the best bootha and card reader in the pind (village). However, since she had not being playing her cards right and close to her dil (heart), she had fallen foul to the wicked rules of the pundits. Hence, she became known as Saali Bruci – played her cards wrong! But it was still nice to see her nice! After a good night's rest, the Sherif of Nott–eating–ham put on his best kameez (shirt) and turban. He put a thick sóná chainey (Chain but not Dick) round his neck and a lovely hara (green) cloak over his modhas (shoulders). He looked very handsome – from a distance. Then, off he went to all the Nawabs who were in Lal Sher (Red Lion) having a drink of chai.

When he walked in, all the Nawabs cheered. This was only to appease the Sherif as they needed a banda (man) to do their dirty work whilst they were away from India – fighting the Cockneys. The Sherif said he would have bought a round of drinks but he said he had been choried (robbed) by Rubinder on the way down to meet them. The Sherif also needed to use their outside lawatory (Punjabi toilet). He asked: "Please get me some chai and kan dana, (tea and food)." All the Nawabs knew he was lying and that he was a besharam (one with no shame). They all just winked at each other, knowing that he had not been choried. He wouldn't still have his best clothes and sóná chainey (gold chain)?

Billy Babu

(There are besharams in every land and community within Valaait (England). There is the biggest besharam of all time; his name is Steve Kuta Richards.)

His favourite song is: "How much is that kuta (doggy) in the binda (window)? Bhonk Bhonk (bark bark). The bann (one) with the baggley push. How much is that kuta in the binda? Bhonk Bhonk. I do hope that kuta is for sale?"

Now the Sherif started to tell them how Rubinder choried (robbed) the rich Nawabs and helped the so called "poor, pind waley (village people)." Above all, how he killed and ate the Raja's deer in hari lakri (green wood).

"How stop him? You not Sherif?" Asked one of the Nawabs (Whose Pinglish wasn't berry good). "If you not make the pind waley, keep the laws, when they breaking law, you no good Sherif to us. Here we doing fighting for Holy Zameen (land) and you must be going back to Nott–Eating–Ham and if can't be doing it right job mate, we be giving vote to the Raja to taking job away from you and hath (hand) to Yorki Ali." Yorkisheer Ali was a very rough sheep shero shayari (sheep shearer).

For all his faults, they knew that the Sherif wasn't two boothad (faced) – he wouldn't be wearing that one now would he?

After the meeting the sherif got up to leave.

On his way back, the Sherif went through German (Punjabi for Germany) and seen a man selling cheap food. He had the name Adil over his stall. The Sherif gave him some advice, which was; he would have more success if he changed one letter on the end to the second place and called his stall… have a guess what? Now Rubinder and his bandey were having the night off, there was a big match on. It was the Lal's playing the Ram's (Liverpula (Reds) and Derbe County (Rams) – for the Hockey championship.

When the Sherif arrived back to his ghar (home), he wasn't happy. It took him longer because he cried all the way back. Due to spending so much paise (money) to get down to Southhall–on–Sea, once there he was only given one drink and no support from the Nawabs. Also, there was a bad report going back to the Raja (king).

All the way to his ghar (home), he was thinking how he would seduce Rubinder to have power over him. Then a plan came to him like a hara (green) chilli hitting the zabaan (tongue) waking all the taste buds up!

The Sherif thought he would have a beautiful, golden, hockey danda made with a sher (lion) head. He would offer this hockey danda as a prize to the banda (man) who could shoot the most goals. The Sherif knew Rubinder and his bandey would hear about this shooting match and would come to try to win the prize. The Sherif would have many of his bandey (men) ready. As soon as Rubinder and his bandey came to the pind, he would have them rounded up. You would never hear him say: "I will buy the next round!" The Sherif used to joke he met his gharvālī (wife) like this: "I went shopping and opened my batuya (purse) and my gharvālī to–be just appeared!"

Billy Babu

Long ago, when pind waley (village people) went to battle, they had no guns or cannons. Instead, they fought with swords, spears or hockey sticks. The Punjabi bandey (men) who used hockey sottiyan (sticks) were also known as the best in the entire world. They could shoot further and straighter than anyone else – the only one who couldn't shoot straight was Vinga Dale (Bent Dale) and of all the Punjabi hockey waley, Rubinder Hood was one of the best hockey shooters. Rubinder could shoot further and straighter than most of India because he had learned this in his gap year off from college (a lot of pind waley thought it was a Gapp mar da (showing off talk).

When the Sherif arrived at his ghar (home), he sent for a banda (man) who made hockey sottiyan (sticks). He told him to make the most beautiful hockey danda (stick) that had ever been seen because he was going to have a grand shooting–match and he must have the splendid prize to offer the winner. The prize would be a hockey danda (stick) with a sóná (gold) handle.

Then the Sherif sent messengers into the pinds (villages) to tell the entire hockey waley (people) about it. Next, he sent for the captain Bhangra walla he was not only the captain of the army but also, like a lot of Asians, had two or more jobs. He ran all the music shows for all the weekend shaadis (weddings). The Sherif told him that he hoped to seize Rubinder Hood at the shooting–match and he must gather together as many bandey (men) as he could.

"We must have two bandey for everyone of Rubinder Hood's bandey there and must be no mistaking this time," said the

Sherif. Everything was arranged and the day fixed (like the Russian elections?)

Among Rubinder's bandey (men), there was a brave young banda (man) named Dalbir of Derbysher. He was also known as; "Double Diamond" because he worked wonders! He had only been with Rubinder for the last two months. Dalbir of Derbysher had a bhen (sister) who lived in Nott–Eating–Ham, she was a servant in the Sherif's ghar (home).

Dalbir would disguise himself and go into Nott–Eating–Ham to see his bhen. One day, she met him with a pale bootha – she wasn't allowed in the sun, due to the fact if she was to become dark, no banda (man) would want to shaadi (marry) her.

"Dalbir you must not come here anymore. Go, tell your master Rubinder Hood that the Sherif means to catch him, hang him upside down and rub his legs with hairy gooseberries in front of his bandey (men) at the great shooting–match."

"What shooting-match?" Dalbir questioned his bhen.

"Oh, have you not heard? There is to be a great shooting–match next Tuesda (Tuesday). The prize is a sóná (golden) handled hockey danda, but it is all a pagal kana (fooling) of the Sherif to get hold of Rubinder Hood. I heard the Sherif through the grape bine (Punjabi vine) talking about it to the captain Bhangra walla last night."

Billy Babu

"I must go. Goodbye," said Dalbir. "I must go back to the Hari lakri (green wood) to warn Rubinder as quickly as possible."

Dalbir hugged his bhen (sister) thanked her and went as fast as he could. When he got back to the Hari lakri (green wood), he found that the news of the match had already reached Rubinder. The bandey (men) were all gathered together, talking it over and already preparing their hockey sottiyan (sticks).

Dalbir (The Double Diamond) of Derbysher, stepped forward and said: "Master, please hear me and do not stir from the Hari lakri (green wood). To tell you the truth, I'm well informed that this match, it is a fix. The Sherif has set this up to capture you, all your bandey (men) and their hockey sottiyan (sticks)."

"You talk like a coward." Rubinder replied. "And why do you say, 'to tell you the truth?' Do you lie most of the time? If you are afraid, stay at ghar (home) with the teemiyan (women). As for me? I intend to try for this prize!"

Rubinder felt so brave that it made him careless of danger and a little foolish sometimes.

Dalbir of Derbysher was hurt that Rubinder should call him a coward. He turned away without another word. Double Diamond works wonders – but not this time!

Within a minute, Rubinder was sorry for what he had said and shouted:

Rubinder Hood Prince of Chors

"Oi! Dalbir. I didn't mean it. Come back, my dost (friend), and tell us what you have heard; is it news all over the world?"

When Dalbir had told them all he knew, they agreed that it would never do for them to walk straight into the trap, which the Sherif had prepared for them.

"Yet I should dearly like to go," Rubinder said rubbing his hath (hands).

For Rubinder longed to have a sóná (golden) handle hockey danda. He had never seen one before, let alone owned one.

"Well, I don't see why we shouldn't," said Lachew of Lawenton (Punjabi from Leamington). "Of course it would be very pagal (crazy) to go as we are, dressed in hara (green). Let's all leave off our hara for one day and dress ourselves differently? No one would notice us then. We could come and go quite safely. One shall wear gora (white), another lal (red) and another neela (blue). This disguise will fool the prize fool!" Laughed Lachew of Lawenton as he slapped Rubinder on the back and rubbed it – this is a Punjabi tradition.

"That is a very good plan; do you not think so Dalbir?" Rubinder added, putting a hath (hand) upon his moda (shoulder). Rubinder wanted to make Dalbir forget his unkind words. When Dalbir smiled, Rubinder slapped his back – everyone likes a pat on the back. There were no pats in India, only in the Eastend with her kaantey (earrings).

"Why, yes, Rubinder. I think it will be very good fun," Dalbir replied, laughing and falling forward. He was very good tempered as well as brave and he had forgiven Rubinder already. Dalbir took the opportunity to slap Rubinder's back to get his own back on him. Back to the start then hey?

"May I come too?"

"Yes, Dalbir, you shall come with me for we must not go all together." Rubinder turned to the bandey and said: "We must go in twos and threes. Mix with the other pind waley (village people) or the Sherif will soon guess who we are in spite of our clothes."

So it was all settled. The bandey (men) had a merry time dressing up and arranging what they were going to wear. Early on Tuesda (Tuesday) morning, they set off in twos and threes to Nott–Eating–Ham via different paths. They were soon lost among the pind waley (village people), who were all making their way to Teria–Bridge, the venue for the games.

Everyone had a holiday. Even the school kuria and munde (girls and boys) dressed in their best and they were all crowding along towards Nott–Eating–Ham's Teria–Bridge zameen (ground).

From his bedroom bindow, the Sherif was watching out for Rubinder and his bandey (men). No hara (green) could he see? He was dreadfully disappointed. He kept saying to himself: "Surely he will come. Surely he will come?" (Even with Indian timing).

The banda (man), who kept order and who'd arranged the match, was known as "Master of the Lists," turned and said to the Sherif: "Will you be coming now please, your honour, for it's time that the match beginning. Everyone is waiting for you and your teemi (wife)."

"How many bandey (men) have come to try for the prize?"

"About one hundred," replied the Master of the Lists to the Sherif.

"Is Rubinder Hood there? Any of his bandey there?"

"Nay (no)," said the Master of the Lists, shaking his head. "Not a banda (man) of his. There are many strangers and a good number of the Raja's bandey (men). But not a banda in hara of Rubinder Hoods," continued the Master of the lists.

"He will surely come?" Sighed the Sherif. "Wait a few moments. Have you not heard about Indian time?" (Means you start whenever).

(Remember: Be wise in the use of time. The question in zindagi (life) is not how much time do we have? The question is: What shall we do with it? This is why Indians live so long, they think so much about time and that sadly passes them byeee).

So, the Master of the Lists waited for a few Indian minutes. Then he approached the Sherif and he said: "We begin now. The pind (villagers) grow impatient. (Impatient is the only thing that can grow out of nothing in time). There are so

Billy Babu

many bandey (men) to try for the prize, if we do not start at once, we cannot finish today. Also, when sun comes out bright, everyone will be fighting to get in shade. They don't wanting becoming darker."

"I suppose we must begin but I thought he would surely have made the effort," the Sherif said, sighing again whilst walking, dejected, towards the crowd.

He took his teemi's hath (wife's hands) and they sat in their seats of honour, just behind the hockey waley (men) as they were waiting to get started.

Then the games were started. It was a fine sight. The vast open Teria–Bridge was looking splendid.

All participants had to complete three areas:

Firstly: Who would shoot the furthest? (Most pind waley used to try shoot at Kuttā Clarksun – he was always making stupid comments).

Secondly: Who could knock the apple off William Patel's head?

Thirdly: Who could shoot six goals, into the mosquito net, past Goga the Goalie? (He was the best goal keeper from Goa – better known as 3Gee. 4Gee was to come soon).

The atmosphere was electrifying (even though electricity wasn't invented). All around, the pind waley (village people) stood or sat watching the game. Whenever anyone hit the ball past Goga the Goalie from Goa, everyone cheered loudly. If anyone missed the target, they groaned. Those who missed the target were not allowed to shoot anymore. They were now down to the last three bandey (men).

Rubinder and his bandey (men) shot splendidly. Only Rubinder and two of the Raja's bandey were now left in the competition. The pind waley (village people) had been going wild all day but now they only cheered when a goal was scored past Goga, the Goalie from Goa. Otherwise, there was a kind of hush all over the field, maybe the world, as they all had their favourites.

All three bandey (men) had shot really well to get this far and now they were down to their last three shots. Whoever scored past Goga, the Goalie from Goa, would win the sóná (golden) handled hockey danda.

Firstly, it was Kāḷā Rath (black knight). He missed, disgusted with himself as he walked off with his head down. The pind waley clapped him all the way to the chai ghar (tea house). Then it was Rubinder's turn and he knew the pressure was on him. Rubinder wanted to win the sóná (golden) handled hockey danda, more so, because all his bandey (men) had come to support him.

The scene was set, and out came Rubinder (no, not that way, even though he was gay most of the time) to a rapturous applause. Even the Sherif was applauding him, not knowing it was his number one enemy. Then there was a kind of hush all over the field; you could hear a pin–du drop.

Billy Babu

The sun was beating down on Rubinder (as there was no News from around The World – who would have ever thought that?) He was hotter than everyone there because of his disguise. As he faced Goga, the Goalie from Goa, he knew to stay in the game he had to score this goal. There was silence from pind waley (village people), and even the animals, no horns from tanga waley (horse and cart people). He stood with his modhas (shoulders) back. He looked straight at Goga, the Goalie from Goa and hit the ball as hard as he could. It seemed to sail in the air forever. Rubinder couldn't see where the ball had landed – as the sun was in his eyes by now. It was only when Rubinder heard the pind waley cheer; he knew it had gone in!

Now the last banda (man) had walked up to take a shot and if he scored then Rubinder would have to go and take another shot. If the last banda missed then Rubinder would be the champion for at least the one month because there were competitions all the time. Rubinder had it all in his favour as the sun was very bright now.

It was Changa Rath (good knight). He was a favourite of the pind waley (village people) and of the Sherif as well. With the sun very bright and someone sneezing just as he was going onto the field to take his shot, both meant possible bad luck. (When someone sneezes, you should wait at least twenty minutes before carrying out any actions because it will bring you bad luck and this is what the Punjabi pind waley still believe today).

Changa Rath went and stood in front of Goga, the Goalie from Goa and tried to see the goals as best as he could.

Rubinder Hood Prince of Chors

As Changa Rath squinted, he wiped the sweat from his máthá (forehead) and cleared his throat, spitting towards the crowd. They cheered him on and they all cleared their throats. Then there was a hush all over the pind. They waited to see if this would go to another round or would Changa Rath, miss? Rubinder was standing with sweat pouring from his whole body; this was due to the pressure of the moment. Then, without any warning, Changa Rath hit the ball and it went in the air, but sadly for him, went over the head of Goga, the Goalie from Goa and Rubinder's bandey went wild! They lifted him up and started shouting: "Hi, hi, hi, ho, ho, hey, hey." This was the latest chart topper from Wood Gora Good Gora.

One of Rubinder's bandey (men) had been standing close to the Sherif, and had heard the Sherif say to his teemi (wife): "It makes me quite gusē (angry) to think that Rubinder and his bandey are not here at my competition and not been caught in the trap that I had set for them all."

As Rubinder was waiting for his prize, he was given the message what the Sherif had been saying. This hurt him that the Sherif would believe that he and his bandey (men) had been frightened away. He longed to tell the Sherif there and then that it was Rubinder Hood who was standing here. He made up his mind, while he was receiving the prize, to let the Sherif know somehow, one way or another, that he had been there!

The Sherif's teemi (wife) presented Rubinder with the sóná (golden) handled hockey danda. Rubinder thanked her and gave her a letter. He said to her: "Please don't open this

Billy Babu

letter till tonight. It is just my special way of saying thank you." She promised she would do that and thanked him for entertaining her and the pind waley (village people).

Then everyone left and all went back to their ghars (homes).

The Sherif had hired "Sat and Nav" to track loki (people) as they left because they knew their way around better than anyone.

That night the Sherif's teemi said to him: "What a nice looking banda. The one who won the prize today and what a player! I have never seen anything like it. Do you know that he gave me a letter to read? Shall I read it to you?"

"Yes, do read it," replied the Sherif – as he pulled the hair out of his nack (nose). He had the nack of doing this.

Anyway, the letter read as follows:

"I'm the hara banda (green man) from the hari lakri (green wood) and it was my day to be blessed. I won your sóná danda for my hara ghar (green house). I hope this doesn't leave you hara (green) with envy… appka (yours) hara environmentalist!"

"Eh! What!?" Shouted the Sherif. "I hope not? I most sincerely hope not. That was the besharam, Rubinder Hood… Hai meh marr giya" (oh my, I'm going to die).

This must have pushed his nack (nose) out of place?

Rubinder Hood Prince of Chors

When Rubinder and his bandey (men) gathered under the hari lakri (green wood), they had a merry time. There was a grand supper waiting for them. Such laughter. They had many adventures to chat about and jokes to tell. The beautiful sóná hockey danda was passed round and everyone admired it. The price of sóná (gold) going up!

Sadly, there were certain besharams (shameless ones) who would steal sóná from the poor teemiyan (women). If caught, they were given a warning. If caught again, they would be sent to Saudi Arabia. Here, they cut off the hath (hands). (There were no flashers in Saudi Arabia – you know why? Because they would have their buttons cut off their rain coats!)

Rubinder said: "I understand the Sherif lives in his own little world, sometimes I wish he would stay there and never visit mine!"

Then Rubinder told them all about the letter he had left with the Sherif's teemi and everyone said: "We wish we'd been there to see his bootha (face)." They all laughed and drank to the health of the Sherif's batuya (purse). They liked others to bring their butuya's and they were good at emptying them!

Chapter Four

Rubinder Hood meets Nikka Johnu

Rubinder had now come to bootha (face) the fact that he would probably have to live the rest of his jaan (life) in the hari lakri (green wood). He was a broken banda (man), remembering; not so long ago ago what his jaan (life) used to be like and how it is today. It wasn't long before all the pind waley (people) soon found out that Rubinder was living in the hari lakri. Those who had been driven out of their ghars (homes) by the greedy Sherif of Nott–eating–ham had joined him. They became known as Rubinder's hockey team because they all fought with hockey dande (sticks).

Rubinder and his bandey (men) lived in makaan (houses) cut out of stone. These were dug out by stone masons who were relatives of the Freemasons. They were given this name due to being "stoned" with any free drink that was available. So, allegedly, it was that the richer and more powerful individuals were, the more likely they would be having these

"Free masons" doing their work for them – they would shake on the deal!

Now, Rubinder had a few hundred bandey (men) and he was training them to fight the evil Sherif of Nott–eating–ham. Rubinder viewed all of his bandey as his gharwāley (family). There was one banda who was particularly like his own dear vera (brother) and that was Nikka Johnu – it was remarkable how they came to meet...

The story starts one winter's morning. Rubinder had always considered himself to be a kind and approachable banda but if and when it came to a fight, he would never back down. As long as the fighting was fair and square, he and his bandey (men) would only fight with hockey dande (sticks). A traveller through the hari lakri could sometimes hear the sounds of clashing dande and knew what it meant – please don't confuse these with Mohan–Rees dancers (Morris's Indian cousins).

One day, all the bandey were told to report at ten in the morning, by the river Ganges for a training day. (Similar to a teacher's training day. Even though they've trained for years to become teachers?)

This was to be ten o'clock sharp and not Indian time. (Indian time is anytime you like but you can't say this because this is not PC and you could be in trouble with the earache equality rights commission). So, they set off for the place on their tangas and on khora–back (carts and horseback).

Billy Babu

Rubinder wanted to take a short–cut over the Ganges River but it was swollen, running fast, and it would be very cold this time of the winter. Gurinder Brown, the minister of AIDS (a term of medieval finance, where part of the service due to a Nawab from his bandey), wasn't giving away any rupees for the winter to keep the pind waley (people) warm. Everyone was browned off by this so called prudent decision. Well, they were as browned off as they could be but not many would notice this. Nevertheless, Rubinder set off to cross the river on his own.

Rubinder came to the Pear (foot) bridge, which was named Pear because you could only walk over it. If you had a tanga then you would have to use the Sarpanchtion Bridge, which was ten kilometers down river. All of the bandey (men) were crossing over from the latter for their training. Rubinder, after looking around, cautiously dismounted and led his khora (horse) across the narrow bridge. He suddenly noticed that a vada (giant) banda (man) was crossing from the other side.

"Oi, oi, oi, oi. (Can you name that Bhangra tune yet?) You! Go back and let me come over first." Rubinder shouted at the vada banda (big man).

The vada banda laughed, and shouted back: "I know my delle (eye) sight isn't too good but I'm sure a keeri (ant – should have gone to Speca–Seva) has said something to me?"

Rubinder was not impressed on hearing this. He could see this banda wasn't going to back down and his bandey (men) were not with him for support. This made the situation rather tricky and Rubinder didn't like anyone playing trickery with him.

The atmosphere had a sense of desperation. As both bandey (men) came closer and were standing angootha to angootha (toe to toe), there was an akhs (eyeing) up of each other. Rubinder looked up to Nikka Johnu's delle (eyes); they seemed to be burning through him. Rubinder said: "Hello, Motto! (fatty)" with a nervous laugh, knowing he was pushing the boat out on this one! (Even though the water wasn't going be under the bridge for him until the fight was over).

Rubinder took his hockey danda (stick) from his pouch, cleared his throat and spat on the bridge. He said: "Look, I don't want trouble with you. If you don't move then I'll be forced to use my danda."

Nikka Johnu laughed and twirled his moustache: "Ha ha! You, a chwa (mouse), you beat me?"

Rubinder's legs were beginning to shake but Rubinder tried his best not to show it.

Nikka Johnu roared: "So you really think you could beat me with your tiny hockey danda (stick)? Mine is bigger than yours and it will snap both your danda and you in half!" (He had been given the name Nikka by his school dosts because he was always nicking their apples or maybe he was just a cross–dresser?)

Billy Babu

Now, Rubinder was truly frightened by this the vada banda (big man). He couldn't back down because if the word of any defeat ever got out, his bandey (men) would lose any respect they had for Rubinder. Also, if the Sherif of Nott–eating–ham got to hear of this, then he would certainly ensure the news would be put around the world via the dakia (post man or post person to be PC).

"Okay, if you want to do this properly, and I feel we should, let's strip off down to our kacchas (shorts) and oil our hockey dande (sticks) and come out fighting. Whoever falls into the Ganges will not have the right of way. Do you agree, vada banda!?" Rubinder shouted.

"You talk a lot for a little chwa (mouse). I'm going to get changed, come back and give you a few swings because that's all I'll need to do. I can then get on with my day's work. I'm going to enjoy giving you the thrashing of your jaan (life)." Nikka Johnu laughed, as he turned scratching his bond (backside) to get changed.

With difficulty, Rubinder backed his khora (horse) off the bridge and tethered the animal on the bank. Rubinder changed quickly and started to walk towards the giant.

Nikka Johnu roared with laughter, saying: "Look at you! Are you so keen to die saala (brother-in-law)?"

Rubinder replied: "I'm not frightened and you are going to regret this day. You will wish you'd backed off when you had the chance." (In India, there is only one person you can "take a take a chance on" and that's Aba Ji).

So, the fight commenced on the small Pear Bridge and as they fought, Rubinder said: "Whoever falls into the Ganges pāṇī (water) has lost the fight?"

Nikka Johnu replied: "I agree but it will not be me. I have a kalāī zabaan (black tongue) and what I say always comes true!"

(I don't speak with a false tongue; ask anyone from the Punjab they will never argue with a person with a black streak along their tongue.)

They'd been fighting for ten minutes, striking blows off each other. The clash of the hockey dande (sticks) was very fierce and they were both becoming tired, both nearly falling into the pāṇī (water). Nikka Johnu hit Rubinder across the legs and finally Rubinder lost his balance falling into the Ganges with a mighty splash.

Nikka Johnu roared with laughter. However, his laughter was only short–lived as Rubinder disappeared under the pāṇī (water). Nikka Johnu fell to his goddey (knees) and looked over the edge with an anxious look on his bootha (face). Nikka Johnu, like Rubinder, was no killer. After a wait, which seemed to take an eternity, Rubinder came to the surface.

Nikka Johnu dangled his hockey danda (stick) over the edge. Rubinder grabbed it with both hatha (hands) pulling himself up onto Pear Bridge.

Billy Babu

"I thought you had doped (drowned). I never meant for that to happen. You are quite courageous for a dana (squirt). If you had not been so stubborn, I wouldn't have kicked your bond (backside) into touch." Nikka Johnu laughed.

All Rubinder could do was look at Nikka Johnu, who was smiling and offering his hath (hand) in dosti. Rubinder laughed and took his hath, while trying not to show that he ached all over, for he knew he had received a good beating!

"Hello, my dost, you beat me fair and square and I agree that I got what I deserved for what I said. I am kāḷā and neela (black and blue) all over now. So, do you think anyone's going to give me their beti (daughter) in shaadi (marriage)? Thanks to you, if I become any darker you know I won't be taken seriously!" (This is still the case in the eyes of some kāḷā dils (black hearts)).

They both laughed and shook hatha (hands). Nikka Johnu gave Rubinder some dry clothes he had in his jholi (bag).

They hugged each other and Nikka Johnu picked up Rubinder telling him: "Maffi (Sorry – but if you put an "A" on the end it, could cost you?) for hurting you but you wouldn't stop hitting me. That's why I had to bash you so hard." A shaken – not stirred – Rubinder replied: "Okay, but please don't squeeze me so hard because I'm really hurting. It's my own fault for arguing with a kaali zabaan walla (black tongue man)."

Just then, one of Rubinder's bandey (men) came by on khora–back (horse back). He dismounted from his khora and ran over to his master. "Rubinder Ji, what's happened here?"

"We've just had a fight." Rubinder replied.

"Oi!" Shouted Rubinder's banda (man) and took off his jutti (shoe) ready to throw it at Nikka Johnu.

"Don't be a pagal (mad), we're dosts (friends) now. Please put your jutti back on, peera cho boh andi aa!" (your feet stink). Rubinder shouted and holding his nose.

"So who is he?" Rubinder's banda asked.

"I don't know."

"I'm Nikka Johnu."

"And I'm Rubinder Hood,"

At this, Nikka Johnu stepped back in amazement as he had heard of this Rubinder but never thought he would meet him. He felt embarrassed for his behaviour because he thought a lot of Rubinder and he appreciated all the good work he had done for the pind waley (village people).

Rubinder asked: "Nikka Johnu, would you like to join our bandey (men)? We could use a banda (man) like yourself and we would feel safer knowing that you're on our side!" At this, they all laughed.

Billy Babu

"I would pyaar (love) to be with you. Besides, I don't have anywhere to stay these days since the saala (brother–in-law), - don't ask me why – the Sherif of Nott–eating–ham burnt down my ghar (home) and the chapatti–chip shop."

"Good," said Rubinder. "Not about your ghar being saara (burnt) down, but the fact you'd like to join us now! I don't know about you but after all that fighting, I need some khaana peena (food and drink). Come Nikka Johnu. I'm sure a mota banda (fat man) like you must need a lot to eat?"

They all got up, rubbing their tedds (stomachs). (Is the plural of tedd, tedds or tedda or teddi? Oh! I can't "bear" anymore!)

(Classic case of say what you mean but don't say it mean, ya na what I mean!?)

After informing Nikka Johnu of their business, Rubinder allowed the new recruit to double mount his own khora (horse) and the three bandey (men) went off to see the combat training that was taking place down Ganges. They took a short cut through the Saralakree (Burntwood) cemetery and heard someone wailing so loud that they just had to find out what had happened. They came across a banda (man) sprawled over a grave. He was pounding the gravestone with his fists whilst wailing. The three of them were so moved that they also shed a tear. Rubinder tried to console the banda (man) but he wouldn't have any of it, so Rubinder asked him: "Who was this banda (man) you loved so much that has gone from this world?"

The banda (man) lifted up his bootha (face) and his delle (eyes) filled with tears, he replied: "It was my gharvālī's (wife's) first gharwalla (husband)," still sobbing uncontrollably. He went onto say: "If, if, he hadn't died, he would have still been married to her!" They all cried even more when he showed them a drawing of his gharvālī (wife).

Time was getting on and "Indian time" is never on the side of Indians, they left him there and went to meet the rest of Rubinder's bandey (men).

When all Rubinder's bandey (men) saw Nikka Johnu, they were very afraid. Rubinder sensed their fear and assured them that he was a dost (friend) and that Nikka was on their side. They all shouted: "Hello motto" and laughed. Little did the bandey know that Rubinder had Nikka Johnu in mind to train them. He had first–hath (hand) experience of how tough Nikka was. He wanted his bandey (men) to be the best. Rubinder knew that Nikka would have to brush up on his use of the bow and arrow; his skill with the hockey danda (stick) was unquestionable.

That night as they all sat down to eat, Rubinder learnt that his new dost Nikka Johnu wasn't only the best fighter they now had, but he was a gentle giant. Rubinder didn't have a vera (brother) but he began to feel that Nikka Johnu was his mota, nikka vera (fat little brother). They sang, nached (danced), held kabaddi (two teams compete with each other for higher scores by touching or capturing the players of the opponent team) and wrestling matches. Well, it goes without saying that Nikka Johnu beat all of them. Rubinder laughed as much as anyone and said: "I would have fought this vada banda (big man) but I have had more fun watching him throw all of you about and kicking your bonds (backsides) into shape!"

(This is a form of team-bonding, but not one I would like to participate in.)

"It's a pleasure," said Nikka Johnu, while holding two of the bandey over his modhas (shoulders) and unceremoniously slamming them to the zameen (ground).

Later, Nikka Johnu finished off six chicken tikka masalas and even ate the balties (buckets) that contained the remainder of khaana (food). The dish of the night was handi gosht (mutton stew). This is a great dish but is not to be eaten by the faint hearted, being somewhat spooky. Usually after meals, there was khaana (food) left over but it looked like this wouldn't ever be the case anymore.

"Well, let us get some rest, It's been a long day and we have to head back ghar (home) tomorrow and also take some more taxes from the vade, lalchi (big greedy) Nawabs. Rest everyone and God willing, we will have a very good raid in the morning. We now have another very big, bootha (face) to feed!" Rubinder laughed as he limped to his tent, he was still in a lot of pain due to his new dost.

From that day, Nikka Johnu would always live with Rubinder. They were to become veras (brothers) and dosts (friends). So, it came to be that Nikka Johnu was to become Rubinder's second in command.

Chapter Five

Rubinder Hood & the Meat Walla

The Sherif of Not–eating–ham was a very offensive banda (although he apparently caused no offence whilst he slept). He treated the poor pind waley (village people) very badly. He stole all their paise (money) and their makaans (homes) and left them to starve. Sometimes, for no reason at all, he would also cut their hair or nails. (For some it was good because they couldn't afford to have a manicure).

When they were up against it, the poor, pind waley would venture into the lakree (woods) and there Rubinder would give them a "CC" to eat (a Chip Chapatti was their favourite). They were all dressed in hara kacchas and kameez (green shorts and t.shirts), and as all good Indians over fifty years of age, they would never be seen wearing jaaraba! (Socks).

Sometimes, they went back to the pind but occasionally they would stay with him in the hari lakri (green wood) and become his bandey (men), even his Saale (brother–in–laws) according to present day slang.

Billy Babu

The Sherif of Not–eating–ham knew this was happening and it made him despise Rubinder all the more. He was only happy when he had trapped Rubinder's bandey (men) and locked them up. He kept them alive in the hope that Rubinder would try and rescue them. However, there were two problems with this: firstly, the chor leader rarely visited the markets and secondly, more importantly, the Sherif's bandey (men) couldn't keep up with Rubinder's array of disguises. Some of the pind waley (village people) knew what he looked like but they wouldn't betray Rubinder because he fed them and gave them choried (stolen) items from the Nawabs. All the same, Rubinder didn't frequent Not–eating–ham, apart from the need for a bit of shopping. There were the melas (fair ground events) to attend. He always escaped unscathed. Oh, and don't forget the buy one and chori (steal) one free!

(One of Rubinder's bande (men) went to court because he believed everything should be "free," when asked what he does for a living; he replied, he was a shop lifter.)

The Sherif was so afraid of Rubinder that he never personally ventured into the hari lakri (green woods) to pursue him. He knew his bandey (men) were no match for Rubinder's bandey. Now, Rubinder's bandey served him and fought for him because they too had had their makaans (homes) and loved ones taken away from them. Rubinder was the one banda (man) who stood up to the Sherif. On the other hath (hand), the Sherif's bandey (men) only served their master because he occasionally paid them and threatened to kill them when they moaned – the worst one for moaning was Mohan Lisa.

One day, Rubinder was walking through the hari lakri (green wood), when he met a meat walla (man). The meat walla was riding merrily along on his tanga, accompanied either side by two servants. They were heading towards the bazaar (market) at Not–eating–ham. He was dressed in a lal (red) linen coat and a leather belt. On both sides of his strong grey kohta (donkey) hung containers full of meat and on his tanga (cart) was loaded to the top. Everything had to be sent by road. The roads were so bad that even tanga couldn't deal with them; the wheels were always getting stuck in the mud.

Everything was carried on khora back (horse back), in sacks or dabbe (containers) but you still had to have a good horn. For without it, you could never get through the traffic. On the back of his tanga, it would say; "Horn please." You can still see this sign all over India and if you do, give them one – that's a horn please – Note: it's illegal to honk anyone's horn!

The meat walla (man) rode merrily along, whistling as he went, unaware that he was about to be confronted. Then suddenly, Rubinder and his bandey stepped out from the hari lakri – they stepped out as they knew coming out can have its own connotations.

"Oi masala, (my brother–in–law or Indian spice), what do you have on your tanga (cart)?" Rubinder asked.

Billy Babu

"Meat. The best chickens and goats for Not–eating–ham bazaar. Are you wanting? If you wanting then you having, if you no wanting then you no having. So, what you wanting to having them or wanting not?"

"Yes, I am wanting, I'll take the lot and your kohta (donkey) too." Rubinder replied back to the meat walla with a big smile.

"What are you wanting them pour, excluding servants of course, Pinglish not berry good please forgiving me." Meat walla laughed.

"I am wanting to go to Not–eating–ham and see what sort of meat walla I would be making in the bazaar (market). Now, I don't know the way so will you let me borrow your two servants to show me the way?"

The meat walla thought for a while: "yes, yes, they can be showing you way to my stall and helping setting up." (But who is setting who up?)

"I will give you more than you deserve! What are their names?" Rubinder asked.

"Sat and Nav (Satvinder and Navinder). They come from a family of worldwide travellers!" Rubinder and his bandey (men) laughed at the meat walla as he walked away giving them the information.

Counting his paise (money), the meat walla went off whistling and Rubinder was left holding the suit of Lincoln lal – feeling very grand indeed. Rubinder then put on the meat Walla's lal (red) clothes and leather belt but he kept his own hara (green) turban on.

Then Rubinder got onto the tanga and off he went to Not–eating–ham to sell the meat at the bazaar. His bandey (men) cheered in the background. They knew if all went to plan that Rubinder would be fleecing the Sherif of Not–eating–ham and bringing back a nice reward for them all. Sat and Nav showed him the way – this could catch on? (Please proceed to the next paragraph below.)

When Rubinder arrived, he found commotion all around the pind (village). In those days, there were very few shops. There was only one post office, this was owned by Mr. Patel. The chemist owned by Mr. Patel. The florist owned by Mr. Patel and an undertaker you guessed it; owned by Mr. Patel's family. (Please don't confuse this Mr. Patel with the news-ajant from Aston Billa – great banda). Everyone used to go to the bazaar, both to buy and sell there. All the pind waley (village people) purchased the following: cooking oil, eggs, yoghurt, flour and sugar to sell. There was no need for toilet paper as everyone had the bottle to do without it! (I do hope that pun not gone down the pan or it will leave me flushed and nothing to go on).

With the paise (money) the pind waley (village people) made they purchased the following items: chapattis, cups, pots and phandey (dishes, or Andy's brother to take back to the pind with them) There were both rich Nawabs and their teemiyan (wives) almost rubbing modhas (shoulders) with humble pind workers as everyone was pushing and crowding

Billy Babu

together. Rubinder found it quite difficult to drive his tanga (cart) through the crowd over to the corner of the bazaar, the place where the meat walla had his stall. This is where Sat and Nav left Rubinder as they had to be recharged.

Eventually Rubinder managed to push his way to his stall, laid out his meat where he began to clear his throat and shout with the best of them. He had brought his own spit cup because you couldn't spit on the zameen (ground). Next to Rubinder was Mrs. Donna–Kebab Akhtar, an SW (sly worker – something to do with needling) and Mrs. Pretoe who was the local chiropodist. Then there was Mr. Allo Wallia, he sold potatoes. Next to him was the onion walla, whose name was Mr. Gunda who had his brother with him – Onion Bhaji. Next to them was Makhan the butter walla. Wandering here and there was some awful chap no one could understand, he sold mutter (Peas). Then there was Mr. Nakk Chwa (nose mouse) who had a nose for catching mice and was often thrown out of the bazaar for picking his nose because he had the nakk (nose). Today he was in for a while – but where? Who nose?

"Best meat teemiyan (women). Come and buy the cheapest meat in all the bazaar teemiyan. Come buy, come buy (maybe, come–buy–yaar?) Two rupees a kilo, teemiyan, two rupees a kilo come choose your own cut. Come choose your own!" Rubinder shouted.

"What?" Asked everyone: "Bakree (goat) meat at two rupees a kilo? We've never heard of such a thing. Why, it is generally ten rupees a kilo!"

Rubinder Hood Prince of Chors

Now, Rubinder knew nothing at all about selling meat as he had never bought any. He and his bandey (men) used to live on what they killed in the hari lakri (green wood). The only ones who actually knew about his book–keeping were; Satpal (his protector friend) and Payingpal (his money friend).

When the pind waley (village people) heard that there was a new meat walla, who was selling his meat for two rupees a kilo, pind waley came swarming around Rubinder's stall eager to buy. All the other meat walla's stalls stood redundant whilst Rubinder plied his trade.

Meat waley stood around, they began to talk amongst themselves and asked: "Who is this banda?" None of them had seen him before. "Where does he get this meat from? He must have stolen the meat and wants to get rid of it quick? He can't make a living like this for long," they all grumbled. "I hope he never comes here again," others said.

"We'll never be able to make a living whilst he is selling at two rupees for a kilo. This banda (man) is a pagal (crazy)," said one old bazaar walla, having been a meat walla for many years. The old bazaar walla continued to talk: "For forty years have I come and gone to Not–eating–ham bazaar and I have never seen the likes of this. I even remember Chapbanda Pincher and his gharvālī (wife) Bheny Pincher from over the sea, he would investigate this banda."

"This banda is tarnishing the trade as well as our meat and who knows how many more will come here like him!"

Billy Babu

Masar Mucha walla said, (uncle with a moustache), twirling his moustache as he moaned.

As the bazaar waley (market traders) looked on they saw themselves slowly becoming redundant and losing all their customers to Rubinder. The bazaar waley were shouting at Rubinder and telling him: "Your plan is very crazy, yaar (friend)!"

Upon hearing this, Rubinder shouted back: "A bad plan is better than no plan. You ask Lord B–liar!"

The old meat walla spoke out amongst the others: "we need to talk to this banda (man) and find out who he is. We must invite him to have a cup of chai (tea) with us and the Sherif, in the Taj Mahal." (In moonlight of course).

The meat waley used to have chai together in the Taj Mahal after the bazaar was over and the moon was up (of course). The Sherif would come and have a drink with them. This was the only way he could find out what the gap shaap (gossip) was all about and who was doing what to whom. It was everybody's "hack" (right) to find and listen–in on the gap shaap. (Some people hacked in too many times).

The old meat walla approached Rubinder, who was very approachable (this was one of his good points) and asked Rubinder: "Would you like to have a nice cup of chai with the other meat waley?" (In the moonlight of course).

"I would pyaar (love) a cup!" Rubinder replied. "I am very thirsty after all my shouting, it has been non–stop all morning and there were so many pind waley (village people) wanting my meat. Talk about Nott–eating–Ham, I am glad there are no vegetarians around here otherwise I may have been a reluctant steak-holder."

The old meat walla motioned Rubinder to follow him. The old banda (man) led the way with Rubinder and the other meat waley followed them.

They all gathered in the Taj Mahal, preparing the chai (tea), the old meat walla was going to do the "CID" (Conjuring Indian Detection). He questioned Rubinder to try and find out who he was and why he had come to their bazaar.

"Is this your first time here at Not–eating–Ham?"

"Yes," replied Rubinder to the old meat walla.

"There is usually another trader at that stall and he never does as well as you have done today," stated the old banda.

"This is my first time at a bazaar and this is the first time I've done this sort of selling," continued Rubinder.

"What made you want to sell meat, and so cheaply?"

"Well I got up today, and thought the steaks are too high for some, and I thought that I would steak out my future in the meat trade, so here I am," replied Rubinder, with a vada billie (big cat) smile.

Billy Babu

The old banda (man) asked: "How do you like your chai, all in the pot and boiled for half an hour, or like the Yorkisheer, wetting the leaves and drink it straight away?"

(How much! A shout you will hear in Yorkisheer, especially from the bandey).

"Oh! It has to be Indian style with all the chillies, masala and every time it comes to the boil, remove from the fire and then put back on. Please note, I only have one day here so don't take forever!" Rubinder said jokingly, wiping the sweat off his máthá (forehead).

They both laughed because they knew it would not be ready until the moon was out. There was an easing of the tension which had built up between them. They all began to see Rubinder as a simple banda (man). The old meat walla started to twirl his moustache just a bit now and not into knots as he had been doing before. Just then, it was announced that the moon was up and the tea was ready.

Just in time the Sherif walked into the Taj Mahal (on what a surprise) and shouted: "The chai is on me!" (A bit like the Milkee Bahar munda). All the bazaar traders got up and cheered him as it wasn't very often they got a drink out of this banda (man).

In fact, they used to say: "what's the difference between a coconut and the Sherif ? You can get a drink out of a coconut!"

Rubinder Hood Prince of Chors

Now the Sherif's second gharvālī Cheriva was there. (His first was named Se–saw, but she left him due to the ups and downs of their relationships).

She was intrigued by Rubinder, especially when she heard that he was the new meat walla, who had been selling fabulous pieces of cheap meat. Unlike her gharwalla (husband), Cheriva was caring, honest and gave paise (money) to the gareeb (poor) pind waley (village people). She found Rubinder approachable, not knowing that he was of the same persuasion and asked him if he would like some Indian sweets.

"Yes, I'd like a Kulfi_Annan," (under nourished ice cream made by the U.N). or Bankey MANGO MOUSSE (New U.N sweetie), Rubinder replied, with his mouth watering.

Cheriva was unhappy when the Sherif called Rubinder away for some chai (tea), declaring that all the masalas (spices) were in the chai now! "It's so nice to meet with you, young munda (boy). Please come to me first, when you've meat to sell again," Cheriva called out, as Rubinder walked towards the chai.

"I will bring my tanga to you first and I must say, thank you for all the sweets," replied Rubinder, putting his hath (hands) together. (This is the way to show respect, or saying, 'Please go. I've had enough.' What do you think?)

The Sherif was sitting at the table with the old meat walla. Rubinder went and joined the Sherif. All the meat waley congregated there with their saara boothas (miserable/

Billy Babu

burnt faces). Only Rubinder was enjoying the chai (tea). He couldn't help but smile to himself with thoughts of having chai with his great enemy, the Sherif of Not–eating–ham, whilst he bathed in moonlight. (It's as good as they say it is?)

The Sherif looked at Rubinder and asked: "Why are you laughing, young banda?"

"Never have a saara bootha (burnt face) when you are sad because you never know who loves you for your smile! Laugh and the world laughs with you, but cry and you cry on your own," Rubinder replied with a smile. This was so ridiculous that everyone at the table started to laugh! They all laughed so much that the tears were rolling down their boothe (faces). Rubinder continued to tell them jokes until one of the bandey (men) with the Sherif stood up and said: "I asked Patel the chemist if I could have some sleeping tablets for my gharvālī (wife)."

"Why?" Patel asked.

"Because she keeps waking up!" Sherif's banda (man) laughed.

The Sherif pushed his banda out of the way and said: "You and your gharvālī (wife), you pyaar (love) her to death. You worship the zameen (ground) that is coming to her! Mind you, he did upset her one day when she said to him: "Look, after thirty years of marriage, I can still get this on." He replied: "It's only a chunni (scarf)!" Others made fun of the Sherif. However, the Sherif didn't seem to be offended because his laughter always found its way to the bank, with all their paise (money).

All the time Rubinder was laughing, he was thinking how he was going to take everything away from the Sherif of Not–eating–Ham. This inspired him. He also wanted to laugh all the way to the bank with his paise (money)!

Now the Sherif, as we have said, has always been a lalchi (greedy) banda (man) and he was thinking: "This pagal (fool) young munda (boy) plainly doesn't have any understanding of how to run a business. If he has any more meat at his ghar (home), I might buy it from him for next to nothing and sell it all for a vast profit to all the other meat waley. I could get myself a nice Indian takeaway every night for the rest of the month!" Indians love to takeaway but not so keen on dividing their gains.

The Sherif was so rude that he didn't ask Rubinder his name; he was so engrossed with making paise (money).

Rubinder had finished his chai (tea) and sweets. The evil Sherif took him to one side and said: "Young munda (boy), I pyaar (love) your company. I want to help you; I want to put an idea to you that will help your new company grow. There will be pind waley (village people) who will try and chori (rob) you."

(The Sherif gestured at the meat waley).

"They just want to see your business go down the River Ganges. If you want my advice, let me come with you to

Billy Babu

your farm-ghar (home) and I will buy all your meat from you, thus saving the haulage trouble."

"That sounds like a wonderful idea. I don't know how to thank you!" Rubinder replied as if he was really excited.

"Oh, you don't need to thank me. After all, I am a Sherif banda (good man). Now, how much meat do you have then at your farm?" Rubinder was asked by the sherif as he was rubbing his mota ted (fat stomach).

"Err, let me think, (this is a good tactic if you want to keep someone's mind engaged with your thought plan) I've got over fifty bakree (goats) and if you would accompany me? Then I'll let you have all of them for one hundred rupees or maybe cheaper? I just want to sell them and go into another business," Rubinder replied innocently.

The evil Sherif couldn't believe his kann (ears). Without further ado, he called for his khora and tanga to be ready for him in the morning. The Sherif would be riding his khora (horse) and two of his bandey (men) would be driving his tanga.

The Sherif's dil (heart) was jumping with joy at the thought that Rubinder had so many bakree, he started to sing to himself: "If I were a rich banda, but but ding ding but ding ding. All day long I'd but but ding. If I were a wealthy banda (man)!"

Rubinder Hood Prince of Chors

Whilst singing to himself he was working out in his demaag (brain) how much he was going to make out of this young pagal (fool).

The Sherif's tale was a classic one of; "You can fulfill a banda's need but never a banda's (mans) greed." All the time the Sherif was completely unaware of Rubinder's plans for him. (Not knowing that he himself was the destroyer of Rubinder's family). Rubinder still wanted the Sherif to pay for all the choriyan (thieving) that he was still doing.

"Munda (boy), I would like to go to your farm and see all your livestock. I'm a banda (man) who has to see it, before I can make up my mind. You know, the only thing I didn't see was the bootha (face) of my gharvālī (wife) but this wasn't an issue because her papa was a very powerful banda (man). Also, I wanted to ask if maybe you have something else for sale?"

Then the Sherif whispered: "And are you on your own, or do others live with you?"

"No, I live on my own. My gharwaley (family) have all gone abroad to work. They send me paise (money) to carry out investments," Rubinder replied.

"Oh, that's sooooo nice to know. I don't want to upset anyone. I'm not one to do such a thing," said the Sherif rubbing his hath (hands) like some of his bande; the Kevsta the lover of free Indian food, not forgetting big T the silent assassin and tight fisted Maxsood.

Billy Babu

By this time, the Sherif's dil was beating faster. He thought that, at last, all his Diwali's (festival of light) had come at once. He began to hum: "I can see clearly now the rain has gone." This is a song by Jindy Nash, a country and eastern singer.

"Well, we can go as soon as you're ready. By the way I'm not very good with numbers. I can't count more than fifty but I can tell you that I have to count fifty times, fifty over and over again. That's how many animals I have for sale. Also my zameen (land) and the farm ghar (home) too." Rubinder replied.

"Well, my dear mithi (sweet), helpful dost (friend). We shall go on in the morning because it's getting dark now and I want to see all the zameen (land). I don't want to strain my delle (eyes) to see what will be mine for a fair price," said the Sherif, with a big smirk on his bootha (face).

In the morning, the Sherif was up first and he went to check on Rubinder to make sure he was still there and not gone in the night. Noticing his prey, a smile broke out on his bootha (face) as he rubbed his hath (hands) together. Rubinder, noticing this (he was pretending to be asleep), laughed to himself, he knew that for him, his dream was about to become reality but for the Sherif, his nightmare was about to begin.

The Sherif had been counting his rupees all night and he thought five hundred would be enough to rip off Rubinder. Now he was going to try to buy everything for two hundred! He had put the rupees in a secret pocket because he knew the dangers of the chors (thieves) and they were everywhere! The Sherif was thinking: "I will take some of the paise (money) off Rubinder by taxing him!"

The Sherif said to himself: "Not only are you so handsome but you're so clever too!" (Some people believe their own lies).

After a meager Indian breakfast (annda (egg) and bread) they packed–up to go. The Sherif took two of his bandey (men) with him to drive his tanga.

It was a beautiful day and it seemed that all the animals in the hari lakri (green wood) wanted to be escorts as well, many of them trotted along at a safe distance. As they started off, Rubinder was laughing and singing because he knew what lay ahead for the evil Sherif. Rubinder knew that the Sherif wasn't aware of how deep he would be going into the hari lakri (green wood).

They went deeper and deeper into the hari lakri. The Sherif, on the other hath (hand), was looking more and more uncomfortable, the deeper they went. He was starting to sweat and was wiping his máthá (forehead), trying to smile. He wished he hadn't carried so much paise money) with him as he had a dodgy ticka. The doctors had also told him that his gharvālī's (wife's) tikka masala (chicken dish) was dodgy too!

Rubinder looked at the Sherif and he could see he was very nervous so he asked him: "My dear Sherif, are you well?"

Billy Babu

The Sherif hesitated in his reply: "Yes, yes, I'm fine thank you but I've heard so many stories of Rubinder. That he choris (robs) bandey (men) who have wealth. I don't want to be next on his list; I wasn't aware that it was as deep in the hari lakri as this?"

"Oh, I'm sure you won't be on his list and its not far now," Rubinder laughed.

"This Rubinder, he has no shame, he will chori you and I, so don't laugh otherwise you may live to regret it!"

Rubinder almost choked trying to stop his glee, and he wasn't even in the club!

The more Rubinder heard the Sherif whine, the bigger the smile on his bootha (face) he was going to make him squeal, Rubinder would savour every moment that was coming the Sherif's way.

"We are nearly there your Sherif Ji, so please don't fret. You will soon see all my animals or should I say your animals and then we can do business," Rubinder sniggered.

"Here we are! All these animals and the farm-ghar (home) are yours. What do you think?"

The Sherif's bandey (men) backed off behind the Sherif.

"I think," said the Sherif (sweating even more, as he continued to talk) "I think I am going to be sick and I should have brought some more of my bandey with me."

"Why do you say such things? Are you not the Sherif of Nott–eating–Ham? The mighty one? The one who is fair to all people, low and high caste? How can I do business with someone who says one thing and does another?" (Just like politicians?) Rubinder chuckled.

Nearer and nearer, they were coming to Rubinder's ghar (home) and some of Rubinder's bandey (men) were now beginning to appear in the trees and peering through the bushes. The Sherif was unhappy because he could see all the bandey in the trees and they were all dressed in hara kacchas and kameez (green shorts and t.shirts), just like the hari lakri. The Sherif's dil (heart) started to beat faster as he heard the horn sound; he knew that this meant he was going to be fleeced. The Sherif still hadn't worked out that Rubinder was next to him on his khora (horse).

Now, horns are only played in the pinds (villages) of India when weddings or other celebrations are taking place. Rubinder's bandey (men) would always blow their own horns whenever they sensed it was pay day!

Rubinder turned to the Sherif and said: "My dear Sherif, why have you turned another rang (colour)? I know we Indians don't like to become dark like the Africans. The fairer we are, the more beautiful we're supposed to be? But you, my dear Sherif, are beginning to worry me. Now have you brought the paise (money) for the farm-ghar and the animals?"

Rubinder tittered to all his bandey (men), who, by now, had all jumped out of the trees and were pulling the Sherif and his servants off their khorray (horses) and removing all that was worth taking.

The Sherif knew he had been rumbled and that this was Rubinder, as his bandey were shouting: "Long live Rubinder, Prince of the Chors!"

The Sherif stood there, shaking in his jute (boots). He saw a very large banda approach him, about two and half meters tall and weighing about one hundred and thirty kilos. It was Nikka Johnu.

"What shall I do with this besharam (shameless one), Rubinder?" Nikka Johnu asked merrily, his laughter resonating throughout the hari lakri (green wood).

"Shall we hang him upside down from one of the trees, roll his pajama (Punjabi trousers) up and rub his legs with hairy gooseberries?"

"Well," said Rubinder to his bande as they repeated the question. "We should make him welcome because he is going to give us all his rupees, khorray, sóná (horses and gold) and his fine kappra (clothes), before he walks back tonight!"

They all roared with laughter and even the animals were jumping up and down.

"Now, come, come, my dear Rubinder Ji (Ji means with respect). Surely you wouldn't send a guest, even though he be a big besharam (shameless), ghar (home) without khaana dana (food) lets feed him? How about panna kuttā (dessert for dogs) for dessert?"

"Yes. You're right, Nikka Johnu. What sort of reputation would I have then? So let's have a feast and enjoy ourselves in the company of someone who has licensed himself to steal the pindus' (villagers) rupees!" Rubinder shouted to all his bandey, who all cheered enthusiastically!

"We'll have something from the Bengal tonight."

"The Bengal?" Rubinder questioned Nikka Johnu.

"Yes, the Royal Bengal. It is buy one, get one free on the extra chilli dishes. So, if the Sherif needs the runs to get ghar (home) then we will help his Nawab Ji."

"You're always the pagal (fool), Nikka," Rubinder laughed with his bandey.

The Sherif of Not–eating–ham was taken into the dina jaga (dining area) and made to sit at the top of the table, as if he was the Raja (king) himself. All the Sherif's kappra (clothes) were removed from him and he was dressed as if he was one of Rubinder's bandey (men). The Sherif was angry with himself because his bandey could have taken this Rubinder the Chor (thief). He had been in his ghar home) and stayed the night! Also, he had been laughing with his gharvālī (wife) and made pagals (fools) of them all. As he thought about this; the Sherif was also terrified and thinking about what they had planned for him. (He doesn't like surprises then.)

Billy Babu

The Royal Bengal (local takeaway) delivered the khaana dana (food) and everyone cheered, even the Sherif was impressed. The Sherif of Nott–eating–Ham wasn't a vegetarian – this was a rumour just meted out about the Sherif but he was a sleeping partner with a very quiet night bed company.

For a moment, the Sherif forgot where he was and really thought he was a "Raja" (king) enjoying the feast. But Rubinder had a joker up his sleeve.

"Sherif Ji, you know how we Indians enjoy a free meal. Well, if you pay the Royal Bengal then we will all get a good night's sleep and please don't drop any of your khaana peena (food) on the zameen (floor). It won't look very tidy with all the bits on the zameen," Rubinder said mockingly. The whole place erupted!

(This happens at most parties. The crispy bits from the likes of samosas etc, always end up on the floor. Check it out when you attend your next free party).

"Please let me go and I will forget that you have wronged me. I am a fair banda," begged the Sherif. "You know that I've got a gharvālī and bandey (men) to feed and taxes to pay just like you. Can we not come to an agreement?"

"Rubbish. You kuttā! (dog)," Rubinder shouted. "I know you have plenty of rupees and my bandey have found all the paise (money) you were hiding on your khorray (horses). We're not chors like you. We request that you hath (hand) over the rupees and the sóná (gold) yourself. So what do you say to that? My dear Nawab Ji? As you're fairer than me, I can't be fairer because I'm out in the sun too much," continued Rubinder with a smirk on his bootha (face).

Rubinder's bandey (men) were already counting out all the riches from the Sherif's clothes and his tanga (cart).

"Please take mercy on me!"

"Like you've taken mercy on all us pind waley!?" Rubinder mocked the Sherif.

"I will give you what I have but please don't harm me and let me go now," replied the Sherif shaking. (No relation to Stevens).

"I won't haaram (harm in Punjabi) you. I just want to make sure you're not hiding anything from us," Rubinder sniggered.

Nikka Johnu came into the tent and put all the rupees and the sóná onto the table. Rubinder started to count it all with a big grin on his bootha (face). Rubinder's bandey (men) walked in with all the paise (money) they had been counting.

"My dear Sherif Ji," said Rubinder unsympathetically, as he continued to say: "I think this paisa (money) should be given back to the pind waley (village people), don't you agree? It's nothing compared to what you've choried (stolen) from them, what do you think my saala, Ji?" (Saala means brother–in–law, it's used as an insult to your enemy. See any Bollywood play).

Billy Babu

"What do you think bandey (men)? Shall we keep him here and for a ransom?" asked Rubinder, as he continued to say: "But then again, they may be glad to see the back of him."

All the bandey (men) cheered loudly and mocked the Sherif. The Sherif was even more afraid when he realized that he was in the hath (hands) of the very bandey who knew exactly how lalchi (greedy) he had been in stealing from the pind waley. Now he was at the mercy of Rubinder and his bandey. He wished he had not come to the hari lakri so lightly protected. His lalchi (greed) had trapped him.

"If I had my way, I would whip you and send you back with just your kaccha (under pants). But as I'm not as cruel as you and you may learn from this, I will take pity on you and give you a chance for the sake of your caring gharvālī (wife). Remember that success is not the key to happiness; happiness is the key to success. If you pyaar (love) what you are doing, you will be successful and I enjoy taking your paise! (money)," Rubinder howled.

Rubinder asked Nikka Johnu to bring one of the kohtay (donkeys). Rubinder wanted to send the Sherif back in style. Then Rubinder's bandey (men) put him onto the kohta (donkey) and he was secured with rope so he would not fall off. All he had to do was keep upright. He was secured facing the kohtay's (donkeys) tail. Rubinder didn't mock the Sherif's bandey (men).

"Don't worry. The kohta (donkey) knows his way to your ghar (home). He will soon pick up the beautiful smell of your gharvālī's (wife's) cooking and when my bandey (men) finally leave you on the edge of the hari lakri (green wood). Don't fall onto the kohta's rear as you may see what you are!" Rubinder said mockingly.

Rubinder couldn't stop laughing while all the bandey took it in turns to poke fun at the Sherif (using their hockey danda), before they sent him off into the deep dark hari lakri. As the kohta (donkey) went off into the distance, the Sherif could see all Rubinder's bandey throwing his rupees up in the air and shouting with joy! (What was Joy doing there? I don't know.)

Rubinder made a parting shot: "Thank you, Sherif. Please come again and we will try not to make an ass of you next time!"

Chapter Six

Rubinder Hood & Raja Resham

When Resham, the Sher Dil (lion heart) returned; the pind waley wept with joy. (Joy would sob with anyone, here she is again). There were bands playing in the pinds and horns were being sounded but this always happened so no one took any notice. It's a pity as their tune was in tune but not with The Tymes!

Now that Raja Resham was back and he had learned about the pagalkanna (tomfoolery) of Rubinder Hood and his bandey. He said to his generals: "I need to see for myself how evil this banda (man) really is."

Prince Javed along with the notorious Sherif tried to convince the Raja that he should just send out a large army of bandey to the hari lakri (green wood) and kill them all. But the Raja wouldn't hear of it. He said: "If there is one thing I've learnt, that is not to take just anyones word. I know how you've been carrying out your enquires but I will go and see for myself and then I'll be the judge of what is to be done."

Rubinder Hood Prince of Chors

The Raja set out at once to try and find this 'so called' pagal (fool) but who were the real pagals? He was beginning to wonder. The Raja went through some of the countryside and Dershanshire where he was advised that he needed to go to a certain lakree (wood) near Not–eating–ham, to find out the truth about Rubinder Hood for himself – in the famous or infamous "Hari lakri". I can just hear Rubinder saying: "informe, informe, they've all got it in for me!"

The Raja with some of his best bandey (men), rode to Not–eating–ham. He went to the Taj Palace, this was a well–known hotel/restaurant (opened by the late Mr. Piara Singh from Balsall, a dear dost (friend) of the late Mr. Babu). He stayed there for one week. When the pind waley (village people) came to pay respect to the Raja, there were free onion bhajis on the ghar (house) and even some to be found in the garden. Also, lots of dancing and singing in the surrounding pinds and even the evil Sherif was contributing by throwing some rupees over the pind waley – though he did have an elastic band attached to his rupees! (Ahead of his time? Plastic money).

(This is the Asian way to show you're happy with the celebrations. It still happens today. The ones that don't want to spend too much use Scottish one pound notes. It looks like a fiver from a distance, but not at an independence party).

The Sherif needed a curry–favour from the Raja. (In England, to curry–favour is to seek to ingratiate oneself with someone in power or authority – or give money to a

Billy Babu

political party?) He also wanted to ensure the Raja never found out he was the cause of all the trouble.

"So, how do I find this banda?"

"He very often comes to hunt in hari lakri (green wood), shoots your deer (oh dearie dearie me) and chori (robs) anyone he meets," replied the Sherif to the Raja, whilst moving about side to side. (I think he may have been be–side–himself).

It was true that Rubinder Hood was the very banda (man) that the Raja wanted to meet the most. Many pind waley (village people) informed the Raja that Rubinder was a great banda and that without his help; they would all have starved to death. This left the Raja puzzled and he thought to himself: "Why would these pind waley speak so highly of him – if it wasn't true?" So, the Raja started to take walks into the hari lakri (green wood) on his own, hoping he would meet this "so–called badmash" (bad man not potatoes). Others, one banda in particular, were hoping that he wouldn't meet him!

Now, Rubinder was told that the Raja was planning to visit the hari lakri (green wood) and that he had been looking for him. So whenever the Raja came into the hari lakri, Rubinder and his bandey (men) used to note his movements but stayed out of the way. They imagined that he would probably be very angry with them for killing his prize deer, let alone the small problem of wealth distribution from the Nawabs; some of the victims were gharwaley (family) or dosts of the Raja.

Rubinder Hood Prince of Chors

Every time the Raja roamed around the hari lakri, Rubinder gave orders to his bandey to follow him and ensure he was safe. For the hari lakri was a dangerous place for some. However, the chors (thieves) were to keep out of the Raja's way. Everyone would recognise it was the Raja as he wore his robe and his mundre (ring).

The Raja was becoming impatient; he called all his top bandey (men) and said: "I want to know how to meet this Rubinder."

He had never even caught sight of Rubinder or his bandey during his forays (I've only known two Rays and that's two, too many) into the hari lakri (green wood). The chief temple walla that worked at the High court was also known as Father Tedd (stomach) of Hoshiarpur (a city) but not of the cathedral.

The chief temple walla explained: "If you were to be dressing up like me, a temple walla, your Majesty, you might force a meeting with him and then you can see for yourself how he treats you and your subjects but you may be in terrible danger."

The Raja smiled to himself and said nothing. Early the next day, he and six of his best bandey veiled themselves as temple waley (holy men) and rode out into the hari lakri. Rubinder's bandey were ready to attack any rich party who may be passing through their territory, and temple waley were no exception.

The Raja disguised as a temple walla, went deep into the hari lakri. Now it was not long before Rubinder and his

Billy Babu

bandey met up with the party. (Oh how he loved parties – but not political ones! This was due to the watch he had bought. It had three hands; an hour hand, second hand and back hand–er! Allegedly, some politicians may wear these watches, from TIME to TIME).

The Raja was a very tall and handsome banda. Rubinder was sitting up in the trees and looked at the Raja coming through the Hari Lakri (green wood) and thought he must be rich to fill such a large frame. Not knowing he was about to be framed. He might have lots of rupees to give the pind waley (village people), rather than prayers. Sadly, there was corruption everywhere and temple waley (holy men) were no exception. (Their leader was Papu Poppy; he could be like a drug for some).

Nikka Johnu stepped out and asked: "Allo Vera! (hello brother). What can we do you for?"

"We are the Raja's messengers and we're looking for Rubinder Hood."

"How do I know you're telling the truth? You chores (thieves) all look the same to us."

(Rubinder and his bandey didn't trust anyone because they were naturally suspicious of anyone travelling through their hari lakri).

"But we are messengers from the Raja," said the Raja as he continued to say: "His Majesty sent us to say he would like

Rubinder Hood Prince of Chors

to see you. As a sign of dosti (friendship) and peace, he sends you this mundre (ring). It is also your safe passage back."

When Rubinder and Nikka Johnu saw that he was wearing the Raja's mundre (ring) on his velvet glove, he stepped back in amazement. In those days, they very rarely wrote letters. They would send a kabootar (pigeon) but the problem was individuals would rather shoot them down and cook them whilst leisurely reading the message over the meal. This led to gossip but when the Raja wished to convey a message, via a servant, he gave the banda (man) his mundre (ring) for authority and sent two Indians – good old Sat and Nav (aka Satvinder and Navinder) their jaan (life) seemed to be mapped out for them by their maa–pe (mother and father).

The messenger was known as the dakia (postie) who was always kept in the dark about the message in the bottle, only the police could have access. Never open it if you find this bottle it maybe an operation Sting.

The dakia, who was accompanied by the mundre (ring), was recognised as coming from the Raja. The mundre was very important to the servants as they then commanded respect and it gave them safe passage. (It was also bad Karma to kill the messenger of the Raja). Everyone knew the Raja of India's mundre. He was known as "Lord of the mundres (rings)," as he had so many. The Raja's top messenger's name was Hari and he had a munda (boy) who would take over one day. He was named Hari's Puther (son) who was destined to get shaadi (wedded) to a relative named Saali. So the wedding cards would read: When Hari met Saali (Sister–in–law – but she wouldn't be one).

Billy Babu

As soon as Rubinder saw the mundre, he knew that this must indeed be a messenger from Raja Resham. Rubinder then shouted out: "God bless the Raja. God bless all those who pyaar (love) him and curse all those who have no respect or pyaar for him, and death to all the witches – both gori (white) and kali (black), who put the black thread on pind waley (village people) and make them slaves to the underworld."

The Raja replied to Rubinder's statement: "Then, you have just cursed yourself and your gharwaley (family), for you are a conspirator."

There was silence and it was not sóná (golden).

"I am not a conspirator," replied Rubinder. "And, if you are not who you say you are? Then maybe we will have a curried temple walla tonight and you would have become the frying temple walla! I do attack the entire temple waley (holy men) as they're bunch of lalchi (greedy), hypocrites who do the work of the evil Nawabs. It will be even worse if you have used the Raja's mundre (ring) to trick me. Indeed, I will be so annoyed that I will make sure that you become a good example to others. But as you live wicked lives you might just get off with a whipping." (They may enjoy this, especially if it's free?)

"If the Nawabs had ruled India well, while Raja Resham was away, we wouldn't be in the position of living in the hari lakri, as we do. On the other hath (hand), if you are just a messenger, I might show my hospitality and let you enjoy the vegetable samosa with tomato sauce, it goes down well in Valaait (England)."

Rubinder Hood Prince of Chors

The Raja said to his bandey: "Come, let us all join Rubinder and enjoy the vegetable samosas, for I am indeed the messenger you speak of."

The Raja said this because he wanted to spend time with Rubinder and find out what sort of banda (man) he really was. So they spent the evening laughing and joking. Most of the jokes were aimed at Prince Javed, the half vera (brother) of the Raja.

As they were enjoying the refreshments, the Raja was trying to work out why his half vera (brother) was so against this banda (man), who seemed so likeable and seemed to be a genuine banda.

"You know, if you were not the Raja's messengers?" Rubinder said, with a smile and a bootha (face) full of vegetable samosa. "We would have stripped you, taken everything from you and sent you on your way!"

As they were talking, more of Rubinder's bandey (men) came to join them. The word had spread that messengers were here from the Raja. The Raja was surprised and saddened to think all these pind waley (village people) had to live out in the hari lakri (green wood) they had been forced out into this situation.

Just as the Raja was thinking about all the pind waley around him, some of Rubinder's bandey (men) came with some deer that they had just killed.

Billy Babu

"Oi, oi, oi, (no it's not the start of a bhangra song). What is this!?"

"It is deer, my dear temple walla, what else am I supposed to do? My bandey need khaana dana (food) to fight the evil Nawabs of India," Rubinder informed the furious Raja.

The Raja replied: "Well, if that's the case, we are hungry as well and would love to join you!"

After the meal, the Raja showed his appreciation by saying: "Hmmmm, this is well cooked and I give my congratulations to the cook. Who is he?"

"His name is Gurindor Ramsi. He loves to ask everyone, chicken tikka masala? (Chicken okay my brother–in–law?) His curries are not too hot and he doesn't believe a banda should cry while he is eating. He comes from the Rams of Derby; they beat West Bromwich Asians in the hockey, this was for the Premi championship. He's better than that Mad Jaffery!" Rubinder laughed.

"Now, would you like some chai (tea) and bescot (biscuit), my dear vera?" Rubinder asked.

"Yes, while I am trying to digest all that information," replied the Raja (king).

"Well now, as you're from the Raja himself, I'm sure you will join in our anthem as we always sing; God save the Raja!"

"Yes, let's do it," the Raja replied, feeling a little uncomfortable because he was the Raja (!)

After the singing, Rubinder told the temple waley: "We would like to show you some of our skills, so you can tell the Raja that we're not just pind waley (village people) out here but skilled bandey (men). We pyaar (love) and would be happy to serve the Raja – that's if he ever wants us to do so?"

They all started to shoot with their hockey sottiyan (sticks) and displayed their great skills. Then Rubinder got up and he shot three straight goals. All the pind waley cheered, even the Raja got up and applauded him. Rubinder then offered his sotti (stick) to the Raja, who managed to score as well.

Everyone cheered again.

"Well. We must be going now, but before we go, I need your answer. Will you come to see the Raja at the Taj Mahal?"

"If I go to see his majesty is he looking for a gap shaap (chit chat) with me? Or is he looking to fancy (hang) me for all the deer I've killed?" Rubinder asked.

"Let me ask you a question. Would you rather stay in the hari lakri (green wood) as a chor (theif)? Or be given the chance to serve the Raja?"

"We would be honoured to serve the Raja," Rubinder replied.

Upon hearing this, all the pind waley cheered, with their hath (hand) on their dil (heart).

Billy Babu

"But how can this be?" Rubinder asked rubbing his thōdī (chin).

The Raja's delle (eyes) were filling up with pāṇī (water). He could see this banda was not the evil banda as he had been led to believe but rather a true, genuine, approachable and loving banda (man). He stood up and removed all the outer garments and the veil. Everyone could see it was indeed the Raja himself!

"I am your Raja, and I am here to deliver justice to you," said a tearful Raja.

When they saw who it was, they all fell down onto their goddey (knees) and held their heads down. They thought to themselves: "What would become of us now?" Would the Raja have them all taken to court – via the Punjab police?

"Get up! I pyaar (love) you all and nothing is going to happen to you, other than you will come back with me and you will serve me. I will ensure all the wrongs done to you will be put right. You have made me so happy. I need more bandey like you, not the pagals (fools) I've sadly left in charge of my rajadom (kingdom). Come, let's get out of here!" Raja Resham led the way.

"Three cheers for Resham the Sher Dil (lion heart)! Burrwahh! Burrwahh! Burrwahh! Burrwahh!" As ever, they couldn't do as they're told but always go over the top, just like the Indian time?

Everyone was so happy and you could hear the cheers all over the hari lakri (green wood). Rubinder and his bandey started to march towards the Taj Mahal, shouting and singing. Now some pind waley (village people) were frightened, whilst many others came out to see what was happening.

Someone shouted that Rubinder and the Raja were going to meet at the Taj Mahal. The pind waley started gathering outside their ghars (homes) to see if this was true.

The Raja soon came to the darwaza (door) and stood there in all his splendor and royal robes.

"I have pardoned Rubinder Hood. He and his bandey (men) have been wronged and now it's time to put things right and move on. In addition, all the bandey who have wronged both you and your bandey will get their day in court and the guilty will be punished."

Everyone was elated when they heard that Rubinder Hood and the Raja were going to deal with all wicked bandey (men) and put them away for a long time. They all danced in the pind (village) with their hath (hands) up in the air and played their drums, singing: "God save the Raja."

The Sherif of Nott–Eating–Ham was now a very sad individual because he was going to jail whilst Rubinder Hood would be free. The Sherif had lost everything, whereas the chor (thief) had gained everything. Also, justice was going to be done by the imprisonment of Prince (good looking – from a distant) Javed, the Raja's half vera (brother).

Billy Babu

Surely no one would ever miss half a vera? The pind waley would miss him – but would like to miss him some more!

Now, ten years had passed by and everyone had been happy, but sadly, Resham the Sher Dil (Lion Heart) died fighting a battle with the communists. They had burnt down his favourite chapatti shop and said: "We've got nothing, but we want to share what you've got!"

So, Prince Javed became the Raja. The governor of the jail had been bribed and promised that he, along with his gharwaley (family), would be rewarded. He ensured that Prince Javed the half vera (brother) was released to take the throne. This was possible because Resham had no munde (sons).

(The Raja did have a test tube vera but he didn't have the bottle to come out – on a gay day!)

Now, Prince Javed, along with the Sherif, hated Rubinder and his followers. There was no option for the former rebel but to leave his comfortable jaan (life), collect his merry bandey (men) and once more take possession of the hari lakri (green wood). Here, he continued to chori (rob) the Nawabs to feed the pind waley (village people) but sadly he was never ever destined to leave the place. Rubinder would sadly die in his beloved hari lakri that he dearly pyaared (loved).

Chapter Seven
The Death of Rubinder Hood

Since the death of the Raja (king), times were now tough and loki (people) wouldn't think twice before they'd rob the poor pind waley, especially when no one was looking because Rubinder wasn't in a position to help anymore. Rubinder Hood had been a dard (pain) in the side of the Sherif of Nott–eating–Ham for a long time. Now, he was in his late forties and he didn't have the stamina to carry on out witting the Sherif and his bandey (men). Also, there was unrest between his own bandey because some of the bandey wanted to retire and move back to the pind (village).

Many pind waley (village people) couldn't tell how old Rubinder was. He wore a very big round turban these days and always had a close shave (in more ways than one). He didn't believe in the myth: "Much nee, kuch nee."

(This means if you don't have a moustache, you don't have anything. This is believed in Turkey because they all think it suits them – even some women.)

Billy Babu

Rubinder was still brave as an old sher (lion). The older bandey (men) were true to him but there were some who had themselves become lalchi (greedy) – this really troubled Rubinder. The one who had always been there was Nikka Johnu. He would never hear anyone say anything against Rubinder and was always within kan (ear) shot of Rubinder at all times.

One day, they were out in the hari lakri (green wood).

Rubinder said to Nikka Johnu: "I don't know what's happening to me. I seem to be growing weak and can't see my hockey ball anymore." (He should have gone to Spek Seva Patel's?)

"Oh! You're just getting buddha (old) my dear vera (brother)." However, Nikka Johnu knew there was something wrong because Rubinder was never ill. Secretly, Nikka Johnu was concerned but what could he do? He just gave him a false smile – like most politicians?

Now, Rubinder and his bandey (men) couldn't go to the pind (village) for any treatment. The Sherif's bandey would be looking for him. No doctor would come out to him; they were too frightened of the consequences for themselves and their gharwaley's (families). There was Dr. Banerjee but he had been banned, he was known as the banner–banda (man).

So they would have to ask one of the chemists and there were only two in the whole of the pind (village). There was Chemical Ali, he was the vera (brother) of some sad man

Rubinder Hood Prince of Chors

(banda) and very lalchi also, he was not to be trusted. Then there was Get–well Patel – who'd helped Rubinder before and was well known in the community. (And does what the community think really matter?)

As they sat with Rubinder, they were discussing how to get help.

"What if we ask Get–well with Patel the Chemist to come out with some medication and check you over Rubinder?"

"I'll leave it with you Nikka but don't put the banda's jaan (life) in danger because, as you know, he has ten munde (sons) and six jobs on the go. Also, he really doesn't have any place to go and call his ghar (home). He doesn't have anyone to pyaar (love) and call his gharvālī (wife) and having both is a blessing. Sadly, he's not blessed at all." Rubinder replied.

"Yes, but you know what the sign says over his chemist. Get–well with Patel." Nikka Johnu smiled.

There was a Witch doctor but no one knew which side he was on. All the pind waley that had been seen by him were ill again. So Nikka Johnu called six of his best bandey (men) and said: "Get the tangas ready and plenty of khaana dana (food) because we're going to meet Get–well with Patel, the chemist."

Before setting off, they had to find a Punk–walla. With all the heat and the mosquitoes, there was a shortage of Punk–wallas. Rubinder did hire a crazy–punk walla, but no one knew of his whereabouts. There was one who'd been in the

Billy Babu

USA (Uniting South Asians), helping the red Indians. It was rumoured he was back but he had to be careful as he had written a song about a rani (Queen) and one was not amused!

Nikka Johnu knew the Punk–walla's gharvālī. Nikka Johnu had sent messengers to ask him if he would fan Rubinder on the journey to get him medical help. Rubinder's bandey had rode out to meet this Punk–walla at his pind – named bhhaunkda (barking). When they arrived there the Punk–walla was out for the count. He was sharabi (drunk). They tried to wake him up and they slapped his bootha (face). He was gone and there was no way this banda (man) was going to come around.

(Remember: There are only two types of honest loki (people) in this world; nikki baché (small children) and sharabi loki (drunk people).

The auntie of the Punk–walla was there. She went into the kitchen and started to cook and said: "I know something that will help bring him around!"

Rubinder's bandey asked: "What are you doing, and, what is your name?"

"My name is Saali."

"Well auntie Saali; your nephew is drunk. We need his services and we need him to wake up!"

"Well, the only way to wake up any Indian is to make thorka," (a base spice mix for a curry).

They all laughed because as all Indians know that not only does it wake you up but the smell will stay in your clothes all day and night! Longer than many old spice(s).

As the Punk–walla started to come around, they asked him his name and he replied: "Johknee Rattan."

"We need your help, Johknee, our dear leader Rubinder is ill. He needs to be fanned as he goes to seek some medical help. Would you please come with us?"

"I would pyaar (love) to help banda (man) but I'm off to play 'God Save The Rani (Queen)' to a raja."

"Could we use your fans for Rubinder?"

"Ye banda (man)," replied Johknee Rattan, who then fell back into a deep sleep. Rubinder's bandey thanked auntie Saali. They took the fans and went off into the night to meet up with Rubinder and Nikka Johnu.

When they arrived at the camp, they explained what had happened and they all got ready to set off. They had to travel at night – such was the fear of being caught. They wanted to be sure no one would see them getting the fans from Johknee Rattan. Some of the bandey (men) had set out on khora–back (horse back) to arrange for Patel the chemist to meet them at a secret location.

Billy Babu

Soon they came to the spot. As ever, Nikka Johnu was the first to get off the tanga and make sure it was safe. Many times Nikka Johnu had put his jaan (life) on the line to save Rubinder's jaan.

Nikka Johnu shouted: "All clear, come on!"

Everything was set out in a circle just in case they were attacked because they'd read about cow-munde and Lal–Indians (cow boys and red Indians).

After they set-up the tents, all of them fell sound asleep.

At three o'clock in the morning, Rubinder woke Nikka Johnu and asked him: "Nikka Johnu, look towards the sky. What do you see?"

"I see millions of stars," replied Nikka Johnu. "What else?"

Nikka Johnu pondered for a minute, and then said: "Astronomically speaking, it tells me there are millions of galaxies and potentially billions of planets. Astrologically, it tells me that Saturn is in Leo. Time wise, it appears to be approximately a ten past three in the morning. Theologically, the Lord is all–powerful and we are small and insignificant. Meteorologically, it seems we will have a beautiful day tomorrow. What do you see, Rubinder?"

"You're dumber than you look – someone has stolen our tent!"

As dawn was breaking, the kāḷā (black) bird was singing but Nikka Johnu told her to shut–up as Rubinder wasn't well.

"I'm sorry. "I thought it would be good for his soul," continuing to chirp but not in the middle of the road. (Not a Chirpy Chirpy Cheep Cheep then?)

Nikka Johnu replied: "Well, you're wrong. He's not a soul banda (man), he is a dhol walla banda (drum man)."

Unknown to his bandey (men), Rubinder's fever was now very high and Nikka Johnu could sense that his dear vera (brother) was very ill. He knew that Patel the chemist was on his way and would be here in the morning. Nikka Johnu was just praying it wouldn't be Indian time! (Indian time could be any time at any day, month, year, or maybe like a Martine?)

Patel's full name was Nilla (blue) Patel. He comes from a long line of chemists. (Have a look around; I am sure there is one near you).

Next day in the distance, they heard the sound of khorray (horses) coming, but they were not sure who it was.

There was spitting and laughter. Nikka Johnu got up and went ahead to meet them. It was Get–well with Patel the chemist.

"Please hurry. My dear vera is so ill and needs help now!" Nikka Johnu shouted.

Billy Babu

"Don't worry, my dear banda (man), I will have him sorted. You know what they say? Patel's the name, making you well's my game!" Patel joked.

Nikka Johnu looked at Patel, he was never this cheerful. Patel was always a serious banda that was only interested in doing a job and counting the rupees. Whilst showing Patel to the new tent, Nikka Johnu was curious as he rubbed his hath (hand) over his thōdī (chin) and thought: "Something is not right here?"

When they got to the tent, Patel took his medication and went in. Patel turned and said: "I don't want any bandey (men) around. I need complete silence and I need to go in on my own."

"No one goes in to see Rubinder without me," Nikka Johnu grumbled.

"Okay, come in with me... but only you," Patel said adha-dil (half-heartedly).

Rubinder was now shaking. He seemed to be mumbling and not making any sense. Nikka Johnu went over to him and wiped down his bootha (face). He was trying to comfort him, when Patel shouted: "I want you to go out! Get my other boriyan (bags) and also get the aag (fire) hot because I need to sterilize the instruments I'm going to use."

Nikka Johnu carried out Patel's instructions. While he was doing this, Patel was lifting up Rubinder from his left side and administering something.

Rubinder Hood Prince of Chors

Just then, Nikka Johnu came in with all the items and said: "Is this all you asked for?"

"Yes." Patel replied.

Nikka Johnu looked at his dear vera (brother). He could see that he was looking very peela (pale) and seemed to be struggling to breathe.

"Can I stay in here with him?"

"No Nikka, I need to keep the tent sterile with clean air. You can see that I have to make a cut to test his khoon (blood). So please leave us and let me get on with my job."

No one was aware, but Patel had married the cousin of the Sherif, who was a gorey (white) witch with a kāḷā dil (black heart). (You've got that in "black and white"). She had given Patel some zeher (poison) to administer to Rubinder. Patel didn't want to do this but she had put kāḷā (black) thread around his neck and he was unable to take it off, Patel was under her control. (You can still see many pind waley with black thread around their necks and not even be aware of it. They can't understand why their lives are so troublesome.) The wicked gorey (white) witch was only using Patel to get into the good kitaban (books) of her cousin. Once she had no use for him, she would dispose of Patel, but keeping his chemist and all the other businesses. (I wonder if this still goes on today?)

Patel had been in the tent for about two hours now. All the bandey (men) were asking Nikka Johnu how Rubinder

Billy Babu

was? However, Nikka Johnu couldn't do anything other than shrug his big modhay (shoulders). Patel could hear all the commotion outside, lifted the tent front, put his unggli (finger) to his bulh (lips) and hushed all the bandey (men) standing around.

Patel tied kāḷā (black) threads around Rubinder's galā (throat) and gutt (wrist), this was to restrict the flow of khoon (blood). He had to do it slowly so he didn't raise any suspicion and to make Rubinder feel sleepy. Patel wanted Rubinder's death to look like natural causes. Now, it was all working very well, the zeher (poison) was working into the cut he had made and the kāḷā (black) magic of the thread was doing its job. Rubinder was so weak and weary that he soon fell into a deep sleep. Patel now knew that the job was being done, so he covered him with all the phurra (blanket) – so he could hide his crime (another way to cover his crime).

Patel then shouted to Nikka Johnu: "Don't let any banda (man) in here for at least two hours and give him this medication twice a day. After a week, you can move him back to his ghar (home)." Patel motioned to Nikka Johnu to pour water over his hands – maybe like Pontius Pilate?

Patel then went on his way, counting his rupees (Indian money).

It was two hours before Rubinder awoke. He found he was so weak that he could hardly move. He opened his delle (eyes) and saw Nikka Johnu there, just like he knew he would be.

"Allo vera (brother), how long have I been out?"

"Not long," Nikka Johnu replied to Rubinder.

Rubinder tried to move but was unable to. He found it very difficult; his whole body seemed to have numbness about it.

"How are you, my dear vera?"

"I don't think I'm going to survive Nikka," Rubinder replied.

"Don't be silly," said Nikka Johnu with an awkward smile.

Rubinder said: "But I saw a kalli billi (black cat) in my dreams and when Patel came to see me, I heard someone sneeze. So I know bad news was in the air."

(A black cat is bad sign and for someone to sneeze when you're going anywhere or when you're about to do something, is not good. Indians won't let you carry out any actions until at least twenty minutes have passed by, or longer if they feel you are useful to them!)

Nikka Johnu removed the phurra (blanket) and saw the kāḷā (black) thread. He knew then that some kāḷā magic had been carried out by Patel and he was furious with himself. However, Patel was long gone now. He picked up Rubinder, took him outside and said: "I'm going to put you on the tanga and get you back ghar (home)."

"No, no, I want you to give me my turban and where ever I lay my turban, that's my ghar (home)."

Billy Babu

Nikka Johnu picked up Rubinder's turban and gave it to him.

Rubinder walked, with the help of Nikka Johnu, to the nearest darakhat (tree) and laid his favourite hara (green) turban on the zameen (ground). Rubinder looked up for the last time at the hari lakri (green wood) and collapsed. The zeher (poison) and kāḷā (black) thread had finally taken his jaan (life).

Nikka Johnu's dil (heart) was full of anger towards Patel. He wanted to rip him apart and hang him in the hari lakri but he said to himself: "I know Rubinder wouldn't want this, he always said to me: You must learn to forgive and then you won't have anger eating at you day and night, it would destroy your today and tomorrow. Anyone who hurts you is the loser in jaan, and in the end, destroying themselves."

For this reason, Nikka Johnu and the rest of the bandey did nothing; they cremated Rubinder and went ghar (home). They scattered his ashes in his beloved hari lakri.

Broken–dil (hearted), Nikka Johnu, the bandey (men) and the animals went back to relay the news to the rest of the pind waley (village people).

There was great mourning all through the zameen (land) when the pind waley found out that Rubinder Hood, Prince of Chors had passed away.

Rubinder Hood Prince of Chors

Patel was very distraught but even more so knowing and realizing that his gharvālī (wife) meant everything to him but he meant nothing to her. Patel had his chemist windows smashed but he was to suffer more at the hath (hands) of his own gharvālī, than he did at the hath (hands) of the pind waley (village people). His gharvālī and her maa (mother) stayed with him till his death. So, just as the poor Patel had been told, marriage is a three-ring circus, it's an: 'Engagement-ring, wedding-ring and suffer-ring!'

Patel's only wish was that he would only have one jaan (life).

(Reincarnation, is not so good? I am being told that over and over again!)

(Remember this fact: The wedding ring goes on the left ring finger because it is the only finger with a vein that connects to the heart).

If ever you go to India, you will still see the place of Rubinder's death and the place of his grave stone. Sadly, as you come off the A-sian38, you are still chori (robbed) by the local government and even the Punjab police. You will know this as they ask you: "Have you got any rupees for chai pāṇī (tea/water)? Unless you Mett the police as you come up from the south, then you may be asked to wine and dine them? The world police could learn so much from the Indian police. You've got to back-hath (hand) them?

On Rubinder's gravestone, you will see these words:

Billy Babu

"We're born alone. We live alone. We die alone. Only through our pyaar, dosti (love and friendship), and prays can we create the impression for the moment that we are not alone. Remember to keep your dosts close and keep besharams (shameless people) closer!"

Long may his name live on. We know great bandey (men) like Rubinder Hood, prince of the chors, are exceptional.

Dear readers:

Message from Billy Babu: "dosti (friendship) and pyaar (love) are like a book. It takes a few seconds to burn it but it takes years to write."

About The Author

Billy was the first member of his family to be born in the West, and the seventh son of the late Mr. and Mrs. Babu. After an ordinary childhood his life took a dramatic change the day he was told to serve behind the bar at his father's pub in Walsall, he'd have to walk back from his school to serve at lunch times and later work into the early hours of a morning. Here Billy learned his trade as an impersonator and joker by listening to all the accents and jokes that came from the customers.

Billy Babu loves to watch people interact and is forever alert to their traits and personalities. This has been put to good use where over the last thirty years, has acted on BBC's crime watch as a robber, a singer with a band and as a solo radio presenter on breakfast and drive-time shows. He has also appeared as a stand-up comedian, a writer and raised funds for charities. He is also known as The Indian Robin Hood.

Billy Babu

Billy was the first Asian impressionist to appear on both ITV and BBC in the early eighties.

Follow Billy on Twitter: @BillyBabu7

Or email: Billybabu@live.co.uk